PORTRAIT
OF SIMONE

PORTRAIT OF SIMONE

ODIE HAWKINS

Originally published by Holloway House Publishing Co.

Front cover photo by Nima Razfar
www.nimarazfar.com

Copyright © 1991, 2012 by Odie Hawkins

ISBN: 978-1-5040-3590-3

Distributed in 2016 by Open Road Distribution
180 Maiden Lane
New York, NY 10038
www.openroadmedia.com

To the power of Echu,
The glory of Oshun
and
The beauty of Alyce Simpson

PORTRAIT
OF SIMONE

Prologue

The southern section of the United States has a peculiar history, a peculiar way of looking at things. The South is our tropical zone, the place where armpits carry half moons and the way people speak reflects a social status that may be missing in the rest of the country.

In the South the recent past may be yesterday or a hundred years ago. People seem to relate to older feelings there than in the rest of the country. Or so some people think. Art, mystery, food, craziness, murky water, dark nights, the smell of skunks, dog howls and deeper love swell up down there and keep the emotional belly fuller than anywhere else in the country. We don't want to get into catfish and corn-bread. That would almost be explaining the whole thing. You meet people in the south that you would never meet in any other part of the country, or the world.

On the back roads in Georgia trees hang over like old men shedding dry tears, and when it rains the earth bleeds, sheds rivulets of blood. Some of those trees have held the bodies of African men and women, their necks brutally cradled in heavy coils of lynch rope.

During the hey day of American-style Apartheid, the South was the African's hell in full view, filled with emotions so raw that they have never healed, will never heal. The South smells different, is filled with flowers that refuse to have color or odor after they are taken from their native soil. The South was once the aggravated land of African women. There is the story of a beautiful African woman who was raped at least once week (from 12 years old to 24 years old) all of her adult life. She stopped the rapes by biting the dick off of her last rapist. The white men of her town, outraged by her rebellion, tied her to a tree and used her for target practice. They say she died with a smile on her face.

The South has always carried this bitter-sweetness for African-Americans. Alone, without Eurocentric prodding or interference, we have sometimes turned the South into a gorgeous place, bursting with an African love system that embraced every Black face in sight.

The South is where the United States sent Leon to "serve his country." The government had no intention of introducing Leon to Simone, but it happened anyway.

The government had no intention of introducing Herb to Muntuna, but it happened anyway.

The people who lived in the area had no idea that one sad day their land would be taken over, twisted into a mad caricature of human activity, slavery legalized.

Yes, the Southern section of the United States has a peculiar history, a peculiar way of looking at things. This is our tropical zone, and it gives birth to emotions that will not bloom anywhere else. Check it out.

Chapter 1

Never will forget it. There were ten of us on the train being shipped to Fort Gordon, Georgia. About an equal number of Blacks and Whites, all of us pissed about being sent to the South, to Georgia of all places.

We hopped off the train and had to walk about a hundred yards to a cab stand. The cabs, three of them, were going to take us from the train station to the bus station, and from there we were going to be bussed to the post.

April 10th, 1962. Hot! Hot! It had to be a hundred in the shade, and humid. But the time we got to the cab stand, carrying these duffel bags 'n shit, we were soakin' wet with sweat. Everybody was cussin'. It was the first time any of us had ever been south and the inside of an un-airconditioned cab, don't ask me why, was our first taste of it. I remember Leon signalling with his eyes for us to take a look at the back of the cab driver's neck.

Right! Talk about rednecks, he had one that looked like

9

a buzzard's neck. Good ol' boy with a wad in his cheek. Leon, who was really good with stuff like this, gave us a tour guide's "spiel" on the way to the bus station.

"Now then, folks, as you can see, on our right, we have the hundred foot high statue of Private Jebediah Gehokum, the last private to volunteer for the Confederate Army."

Thank God the bus station was air conditioned and it wasn't segregated. I guess that had to do with the fact that it was practically owned by the Army. Somebody told us to sit and wait for the bus to the fort. The bus was due an hour later. We waited impatiently, you know how young dudes can be. After fifteen minutes or so, Leon and one of the white dudes, I think his name was Amchuck or something like that, decided to take a lil' stroll.

"Hey man, if the bus comes while we're gone, tell 'em to wait, we'll be back in a bit." That was typical for Leon. He simply refused to conform. I know what I'm talking about. We went through basic training together. At one point I thought they were going to throw his ass in jail for outright nonconformity. Can you really understand where I'm comin' from? Take my word for it, the Army, like most other big time regimentation systems, doesn't like a lot of non-conformity. And Leon was strictly a non-conformist. But that's besides the point, we were draftees and so far as the regular Army types were concerned, all draftees were non-conformists.

But that's another story. I'm getting ahead of my myself. He and Amchuck, it was Chuck-something or other, decided to take a lil' stroll. Now, check it out, you've got to remember this was 1962 and the bus station was situated in the white section of town, which meant that Leon, the reluctant draftee brother and Elchuck, the "liberal" white boy, were going for a walk on the white side.

About twenty hot minutes later they were escorted back

10

to the bus station by two huge MPs. The military police left with one word. "Stay!" they said and marched back out. Elchuck was red in the face and Leon looked like he was ready to strangle somebody. I didn't get the story of what had happened until we got on the bus, and I got it from Elchuck. Leon was still too mad to talk.

"Well, what happened is that we were just walkin' down the main street, it's called Broad Street on this side of town, and these two MPs popped out of nowhere, puts handcuffs on us, takes us to the local station house and they give me this big racist fuckin' lecture. I don't know what they said to Leon.

"'Look,' they says to me, 'You're in white man's country now, we don't want you to fuck things up by hangin' out with niggers, understand?!'" Hey what could I say? I nodded my head like I was in agreement. Hey, what could I do? Did you see the size of those fuckin' apes?!

Fortunately, Leon and I got posted to the same unit, the 95th Civil Affairs Headquarters; we were, would've been the people to set up a government, if our government had taken over Cuba or wrapped Russia into a knot or something. Two weeks after we got into the unit he told me what had happened to him during their fifteen minute walk.

"The motherfuckers threatened to kick my ass for resisting arrest if I said a backwards word and a whole bunch of other racist shit. Needless to say, I talked back. 'No, fuck it!' I argued. I asked them how they could justify Jim Crowin' me in uniform. 'Like, hey, we're both in the same fuckin' army. What am I doing wrong? Is takin' a fuckin' walk down the fuckin' street wrong?!'

"I asked them. They didn't have an answer for that. In addition to everything else, both of the motherfuckers were from 'way up North, like Montana and Minnesota, and they didn't feel super secure about their racism. Anyway, to make

11

a long story short, they laid it out for me, no integration, period.

"Look, we know you just got here and you may not know what the rules are but we're here to enforce the rules and the rules are, no integration." That's what they ran down to me and then shot us back to the bus station.

We settled into the life in the 95th Civil Affairs unit. Leon seemed to settle into life outside it. He told me one day, about a couple weeks after we'd been given our permanent assignments, "I think I'm gonna hang out on post 'til the end of my number man, I don't wanna be forced to deal with outrageous segregation. Chicago is bad enough." It was hard to believe but he really meant it. Don't get me wrong, I was severely pissed myself. I mean, you from Des Moines, Iowa. But my feelings were, hey, just play the game for twenty months and then get on about your life. That wasn't the stuff that Leon was made of. He wasn't going to go for accommodation on any level. So, while the rest of us changed clothes every evening, tipped into town to track down loose body, booze, gamble or whatever, Leon as promised, hung out on post, draining the library or playing drums at the various post service clubs and going to the movies. I never met a dude who loved movies more than he did.

He held out for about three months and then, without a lot of fanfare, he joined our little group for a trip into town. He made us feel real funny, kinda quietly, if you want the truth. I mean, here we were, six of us, Steel from the Virgin Islands, McKinnon from Phili, Bussey from New York, Da Loma from Boston, Maxwell from "Ell-A" and myself, and we hadn't done anything to try to de-Apartheid our situation. To be truthful, we had just simply settled into it and said, Fuck it, we'll go back on the offensive when we get back on our own turf.

Now, we hadn't boycotted the town, resisted, or done any

such thing. We had been in town twenty minutes. We deserted Steel, McKinnon, Bussey, Da Loma and Maxwell, who were off looking for something a bit more lively than music, and set up at the DeSoto Club. The DeSoto was where they had Miles Davis and John Coltrane on the jukebox. I don't think I've ever experienced anything like it in my life, hanging out that night with Leon. He sat up there on that barstool, sipping straight gin (you ran your own risks when you asked for a mixed drink) and sucked the Coltrane-Davis sound up like a stone freak.

"Man, you now something," he says to me at one point. "I'm afraid for jazz. It's such a precious music."

"What're you afraid of?" I asked him.

"I'm afraid white folks are goin' to claim it."

This, light years before the Blues Brothers and stuff like that. 1962, remember? But Brubeck, Baker, Belushi and a Biderbecke had already done their damage. On cue, we stumbled out into Gwinnett Street with the rest of the love-lost legions and took the bus back to the post. The dude was so political, he actually used to piss me off.

"Hey, man," he'd throw out at me, "you got any idea how much these people who work on this post make?"

"Uhhh, naw, home," I answered him on one occasion.

"$2.50 an hour," he told me. Well, okay, shit, $2.50 an hour, what the hell did that have to do with us soldiers? The civilian employees coming up on the post were earning a dollar and a quarter more than they would've earned if they hadn't been working on government property. That's what I related to. In any case, the brother started going to town with us. He'd hang out, after we got to town, for a half hour or so, and then he'd trip off to the DeSoto to dominate the jukebox until the club closed. For those who didn't dig Bird, Billie, 'Trane 'n Miles, so sorry, too bad. He discovered the library three months after he discovered the DeSoto Club

13

and I'm sure the DeSoto patrons will always be grateful. The man defied Ritual.

"Where you going, man?"

"To the library."

"Where?"

"To the library."

"For fuckin' what?"

"Wanna come with me?"

The ritual was to pull into town on the bus (unless you knew a non-com or an officer who wanted to run the risk of being seen with one of the 'untouchable' types) and cast off, period. Here we had this maniac tripping off to the library. I liked the dude, but his library thing seemed eccentric, even to me. It took him three months of going back 'n forth before he revealed that the attraction was.

"She's really beautiful, Herb, really and truly beautiful."

"Who?"

"Simone."

"Simone?"

"Yeah, the librarian."

It got to be sort of an in-joke amongst our gang.

"Where's Leon, Herb?"

"He's visiting the librarian."

One afternoon, out of sheer curiosity, me and Maxwell, half loaded on some Thai stick his sister had sent him, decided to take a look at the librarian. The library was almost empty, save for Leon, leaning across the front desk talking to the librarian and a few school kids. He frowned when he saw us walk in.

"Can I help you gentlemen?" she asked. Leon maintained his frown.

"They don't need any help, these are friends of mine."

She leaned across the desk and shook our hands. "Welcome to the library. Let me know if I can help you find something." She had this really throaty voice, musical, with this lilting accent. She sounded almost Jamaican. And was fine. If my jaw went half as slack Maxwell's, I'm sure both of us must've looked like complete idiots.

I mean, the sister was fine. From what we could see from the waist up, she was gorgeous. Beige colored sister, dimples in her cheeks, one of them really African pairs o' lips on her, little pixie-curly hair cut, beautifully molded tits, tiny waistline. One of the school kids called her over for something and we got a chance to check out the rest of her. Lush African buttocks on her, not too large or wide. Lush.

"Get the fuck outta here," Leon growled at us.

"Hey, we're your partners, remember?"

"You heard me, get outta here."

Since he seemed to be somewhat serious and hostile, we waved goodbye to the librarian and started out.

"Do you men have library cards?" she called out to us.

"We'll get one next time, thank you." We laid shit eatin' grins on Leon, to let him know that we were honoring his request. His frown lessened somewhat. "See you later on, brotherman."

"Yeahhh, later on."

We stutter-stepped back out onto Gwinnett Street. Half way up the block Maxwell pulled me to the stop by placing his big paw on my shoulder.

"Mannnnn, did you see that sister?"

"Yeah, Maxwell, I saw her." We continued our stroll to the Top Hat, one of three clubs in "our" section of town, talking about what was then called, "a major league fox." The secret was out, now we knew why the brother just had to spend so much time in the library. If the truth be told, we were all a little bit envious of the dude. Who wouldn't be?

The Top Hat was celebrating somebody's birthday and the rest of the members of our circle, Steel, McKinnon and

Bussey were in weekend form.

"Hey, Maxwell! Herb! C'mon over here! Pull up a squat down! Have a drink! Lemme introduce you to...to...What did you say your name was, honey?" We got halfway into the spirit of things after a bit, but from time to time, Maxwell would catch my eye, roll both eyes to the ceiling as though he were ecstasy. We understood.

"Where's Leon?!" someone asked, midway into our third fifth of Canadian Club. Maxwell gave me one of his ecstasy looks and announced to no one in particular, "Wherever he is, I wish I was there, too." The secret was out, to at least two of us, at any rate. Our pal Leon had discovered a gem in the public library.

Chapter 2

Three weeks after Maxwell and I had discovered Leon's reason for staying in the library 'til closing time as often as he could, his war with the Army came to a boiling point.

"Damn these fuckin' bastards!"

I looked up from spit-shining my boots to try to get a fix on the brother's anger. "What's happenin', man, you act like somebody just took your weekend pass away."

Leon stared at me with something resembling hatred. "How did you guess?"

'They did?'' I suddenly felt like a stupid jerk.

"Yeah, that's exactly what they did." He flopped down on his bunk, steam blowing out of both nostrils.

"What happened?" I put the boots aside.

"Well, you know how much trouble I've been having with Sergeant Shearing . . ."

"Yeah, I know." Everybody knew. Sergeant Shearing had been one of the first to come to grips with Leon's

17

uncommitted life in the military. We had all heard him say to Leon, at one time or another, 'You better shape up or else I'm gonna see that your ass is locked up.'

"The motherfucker withdrew my pass for the weekend."

"Awww mannnn, what a drag." It wasn't hard to be sympathetic to someone who'd had their weekend pass removed. "What're you going to do about it?"

"What can I do? Go AWOL?"

We let it drop. What could you do? I went back to spit-shining my shoes.

"Herb, I need to ask a big favor of you, man. I couldn't ask this of anyone but you."

I'm sure, if we had memories capturing memories in those days, I would've seen myself as a hip square. "What do you want me to do, Leon?" He looks ill at ease, a new posture for the usually assertive Leon.

"Okay, check it out, I have a date with Simone tomorrow afternoon and I want you to sub for me." We stared at each other for a long time.

"Why me, home?"

"'Cause its important to me, Herb, this woman means a lot to me. We...I've been trying to set up a date with her for months and she's finally agreed, tomorrow afternoon. You don't know what this means to me, man." He was obviously serious. The truth of the matter is that I had no interest in subbing for anybody. I was involved in some pretty heavy action myself with a dazzling young sister named Muntuna. We were on the verge of making a decision about us, about whether or not we were going to become lovers or just keep on kissing each other into distraction. Tomorrow afternoon was going to be as likely a time as any for it to happen.

"Well?"

"Okay, Leon, just for you." I really felt like saying no

because it wasn't going to do me the slightest bit of good to be out with somebody else's woman. 'Specially Leon's. He'd made it absolutely clear about what his feeling were. "Why couldn't you just call and break the date?"

Leon sighed and laced his hands behind his head. "It ain't that easy with a woman like Simone, man, you have to be careful. She looks like a woman, she acts like a woman, she walks like a woman, but she breaks like a little girl.

"It took me this long to seduce her into agreeing to go out with me. I've been trying to 'further the process,' as they say, which means that I have her at a certain point. If she isn't taken out tomorrow, somehow, she'll be back at the frightened fawn stage and I'll be trying to convince her all over again."

"Convince her of what?"

"That all men aren't calloused, unfeeling brutes who whisper filthy suggestions into sister's ears after Sunday services."

"Is that what you were going to do tomorrow?"

"Yeahhhh!"

I could tell from the disgusted expression that he was terribly pissed. We were pretty well tuned to each other, psychologically and it was obvious that the librarian had taken a big cut on the dude's feelings.

"So, you want me to further your process, huh?"

"You got to Herb. Nobody else could do it but you. Most of the dudes in this unit are pretty much the kind of calloused brutes I been talkin' about." I was flattered and agreed to be his alter ego. The deal was sealed with handshake. He sat up on the side of his bunk and started telling me what I had to do for him.

Three hours later, with a candle lit on his footlocker and a half fifth of Bristol Cream sherry twinkling in the candlelight, he's still telling me what I had to do with Simone.

"Whatever you do, man, don't make fast movements around her. She has this strange notion that people who make fast movements are up to no good." He accepted my stares with good humor. "Yeah, I know, it sounds weird. She's so sensitive."

I had shined all of my shoes, polished my brass and done a half dozen other bits of shit that they used to have soldiers do, listening to Leon.

"I can't really explain it to you, Herb. She's different. Yeahhh, I do want the pussy, I'm not gonna lie about that, but I don't want to harm her in the process. She's precious."

By the time we turned in for the night I felt I had a firm fix on what I was supposed to do to 'further' Leon's process. I was supposed to meet her in the parking lot in the back of the library and take her to this little Chinese greasy spoon that everybody thought was so fabulous. And there we'd talk on a list of subjects he'd given me.

"Leon, I don't believe this. I don't understand why you simply can't cancel 'til you get your pass back. What if she digs me?" I joked. He bristled.

"She better not. And you better not either. But that's not even likely to happen. You're just going to be my spokesman for a few hours. There's no harm in that and it'll prevent her from retreating and forcing me to start at square one again."

By the time he let me turn over and go to sleep I felt as though I had been entrusted to do some giant psychological stuff on his behalf. Real big stuff. I was supposed to aid his case.

"She wants to talk about love, eroticism, free livin', how to enjoy life, but she doesn't know how to. She isn't just a horny librarian, Herb, she's a creature whose been almost deprived of her senses. Bottom line, I want you to tell her, to convince her thata everythang is everythang. She' been trying to equate what feels good with what's wrong. She's not a prude, you understand, she's been shown too many anti-VD films to be a complete prude, but..."

"But what?" You may as well spin the whole thing out to me."

"Well, okay, lemme give you an example of what I'm dealin' with. Her husband's been dead for two years now, right?"

"Right."

"She hasn't had sex with another man since his death."

"Are you pullin' my leg?"

"I wish I was. That's what she told me and the lady does not lie. But that's not what I wanted to tell you. We got into a talk about oral lovemaking or rather, she started talkin' to me about it. This is an example of what I've been dealin' with. 'Leon, do you think that making love with your mouth is bad?' she asked me. 'Are you talking about oral sex," I asked her. I wanted to make certain we were both on the same wavelength. 'I suppose that's what you could call it.'"

"What did you tell her?" I was becoming fascinated by the twists and turns.

"Well, I told her that I didn't think any kind of love was 'bad,' if it wasn't harmful to the people involved. 'How is it done?' she asked me. It took about a half hour for me to really get through it."

"You gave her the whole story, huh?"

"I had to. And do you know what she said?"

"No, what?"

"'I think I'd like to try oral love making sometime.' When, I pressed her, 'I don't know, some day.'"

"How far...uhhh, how, what's been happenin' with you two? I mean..."

"Ain't nothin' been happenin', that's what I want to change."

Like I said, by the time I turned over to go to sleep I felt that I had a real job to do the following day.

Muntuna wasn't too happy about me breaking up our Saturday kissin' 'n feelin' session. "Herb, I thought you was gonna spend this Saturday with me?"

"I was, I mean, I wanted to but I forgot that I had promised a friend that I was going to do him a favor."

"So, doin' some friend a favor is more important than seein' me?"

"Not exactly, sweetheart." Muntuna could be so exasperating when she wanted to. I supposed that was one of her attractions. We came to a kind of truce, meaning that she was highly pissed about me not keeping our date. "Muntuna, I'll talk to you later on. I love you."

"That's what you say, I don't believe a word of it." I knew I'd have some fence building of my own to do, by next weekend. Meanwhile...

I really felt sorry for Leon when he put me on the bus to town, to have this Cyrano-type meeting with his lady. "That's about it, man. That's about as much as I can tell you about her. She's delicate, you know what I mean?" I nodded, yes, yes, I understand, for about the umpteenth time. Yeahhh, I really felt sorry for the brother. We had discussed the ins and outs of him just saying to hell with it! and going AWOL, but I had persuaded him not to go that route.

"Hey, look at it objectively, Leon. Shearing is definitely snappin' at your ass. That's all he'd need to throw you in the stockade for six months, maybe longer. And remember, that's bad time."

He fluxed hot and cold about it, 'till the last minute. We exchanged through-the-bus-window waves. I was off to do something I never thought I'd be doin', going to bat for another dude. Bussing into town, past the green fields, the blood red shoulders of the Georgian highways, the shack-homes of my brothers and sisters, I thought about what it was all about, where we were, "what it all meant," as brother Bussey, our Bed-Stuy-New-Yawk philosopher used to put it.

"What it all meant," Bussey would say, usually at some crucial point during one of the weekends that no one would ever be able to label. 'What it all meant could be usually meant as a non-definition of what was goin' on. The squares usually took the statement to mean that he was referring to the present, to something that was currently happening, but it wasn't like that. 'What it all meant' was a co-ancestor to 'everythang is everythang.' And only a few of us took some pride in trying to understand that.

Wild fantasies paralyzed my head for a couple of miles. What if Simone falls in love with me? I had seen the woman and she was an absolutely gorgeous woman, any fool could see that. What if I fall in love with her?

The lumpy moving bus was suspended in mid air for a half mile of romantic thinking. What if? What if? What if? The bus was stirring dust up on Gwinnett Street before I realized that I had daydreamed myself into town. There was an interesting process about the segregation shit. The Blacks were dropped off first on the way into the white section of town and picked up last on the way out of town. What it meant was that we would have equal access to seats on the way into town but since the bus made its departure from Broad Street, the white boys occupied the seats going out of town. That whole number changed one night when the bus picked up a crazed bunch of us Northern brothermen who forced all the white boys to stand up 'till we arrived at the post. The bus driver, a mainstream cracker, flicked his eyes around like an iguana, trying to figure out why white men would stand up in the aisles for fifteen miles. What he didn't want to understand was that we had offered these white

23

boys an ultimatum. Stand with us or get your ass whipped in your seat.

On another occasion, we sat in the laps of white boys all over the bus, none of them objected and one of them even said something like, 'Hey, I can really understand where you dudes are comin from.'

I had to walk four blocks from the bus stop to the library. It was hot. It always seemed to be hot in Augusta. And humid. I had half moons under my armpits after a block. A half block away, I started working a little review through my skull. 'Whatever you do, man don't make fast movements around her. She has this strange notion that people who make fast movements are up to no good.' 'Remember, Herb, she's delicate, fragile.' 'Encourage her to bump heads with you, she's in need of a book that will talk back.' 'Make her understand how I feel about her, Herb.'

'How do you feel about her, Leon?'

'She's got my nose wide open, brother, wide open.'

'What's that really mean?'

'It means I love her.'

I was walking around the side of the building to the parking lot. Damn! I wonder if I should've stopped off to get her some flowers. She was sitting in a late model car, the only one in the lot, her head bent over a book, waiting for Leon. 'Why don't you call her up and cancel your date 'til next weekend?' 'I can't, man, I just can't. She expects me to pull her out of her humdrum and that's what I'm going to do, even if I have to use you to do it.'

Slow, slow, don't shake her up.

"Uhhh, good afternoon. My name is Herb. I'm a friend of Leon's." She looked up from the book and seemed shiver. He was right. She is delicate, her reactions almost fawn-like.

"Uhhh, yes, I remember you. You came to the library one evening—with another man." She released a neutral

24

smile and bent her head back over the book.

"Something interesting?"

"Well, you know Achebe is always interesting." Chinua Achebe? Leon had led me to believe that the lady was some kind of romantic reading fool.

"I've only read one book by him, I think it was called *Things are Apart*."

"The title was *Things Fall Apart*."

I stared into her eyes. It was always intriguing to me, to stare into the eyes of African people with different colored eyes. The high noon sun caught gray flecks, gold, and mixed them with large platters of cocoa brown. "Uhhh, yes, that's right. I remember now." She was the librarian. She'd remember any title. I felt awkward, leaning down to talk with her. "Uhhh Mrs . . . ??"

"You may call me Simone, everyone does."

From somewhere far away, someone laughed. It was Saturday afternoon and, for some reason, people seemed to do a lot of laughing out loud on Saturday. The laughter got louder at night. "Uhh, Simone, I'm here on Leon's behalf."

She slowly closed the book, staring at it in an odd way. She turned to me with the same odd look, asking questions without saying a word.

"Do you mind if I sit in your car? I want to talk to you about Leon." She nodded yes and leaned over to open the passenger's side. I walked around slowly, carefully reminding myself that I shouldn't make quick movements. I slowly slid into the passenger's seat, sniffing at the new car smells. She turned to face me with a neutral expression on her face. "Leon couldn't make it," I blurted out, "They held his weekend pass up."

Her face sank a tiny bit, the eyes darkened. "What happened?"

"Oh, it's a long story, almost a primitive story, really,

about an enlisted man and his sergeant."

"Is he in real trouble?"

"I don't think so, not yet anyway."

"And he sent you to act as a replacement?"

"Ahem, well, not exactly; well, what I'm doing, what he asked me to do..."

"He asked you to talk to me, to cool me out, so that I wouldn't retreat. Isn't that what he wanted you to do?"

I was stunned. Damn! Is this the 'fawn/fragile female' who needs stroking. "To be honest, not totally. But I have to be honest with you, he did ask me to say some things to you that he wanted to say..." The amused expression on her face made me feel nervous.

"Go on, let's hear how you'd say what he wanted to say." We tried to keep straight faces for a few beats before dissolving into laughter. Her laugh, like her voice, was lilting, musical.

"What am I laughing about? Seems like the joke is on me."

Herb, the joke isn't really on anybody. It's just the absurdity of the situation that's so comical."

"Yeahhh, I guess you're right. What could be funnier than this?"

"Well, I could think of a few things, if I wanted to." I was quickly becoming aware of how much the amused expression was naturally a part of her personality. "I think it would be kicks to listen to what you think. Have you had lunch yet?"

"No, I was waiting for Leon, remember?"

"I remember. And I also remember that I'm acting as his deputy today. May I invite you to lunch?"

"You may."

"How about...how about some Chinese food?"

"Wong's is just a few blocks from here."

Chapter 3

There were two Chinese restaurants in the "colored" section of town, Wong's, and the one that we all called "the other Chinese restaurant." Wong's was bad enough. I can't begin to imagine how much worse the other place was. The place looked good outside and inside, but the food was terrible. I always had the feeling that most of us who knew a little about Cantonese food went to Wong's as a joke, a way of making fun at food that was almost the antithesis of good Chinese food. Number one, most of the items on the menu were greasy. Real greasy at times. Number two, they had a tendency to overcook stuff. The greens, for example, were cooked the way most Black people cooked greens back then...a long time.

Anyway, off we go to Wong's...

I felt an odd sense of respect flow out to us as we entered. It was definitely a different kind of reception from the ones I had received when I ran through there with Rhodessa,

Danielle or Muntuna, even.

"Afternoon, hi'yall this hot afternoon?"

There was Papa Wong, Momma Wong, brother Wong, sister Wong and two baby Wongs. We could never figure out who the six-seven year old belonged to. And we didn't feel free to ask. The Chinese occupied a real hairy step on the segregation ladder. They weren't Black and they weren't White and that's the way they acted. Maybe it had something to do with the times, this was, remember '62 through '64.

I remember a conversation that Bussey (our resident intellectual from Bed Stuy, New York) and I had with Brother Wong one bleary evening. We were trying to make a slightly narcotized decision about the stuff on the menu (Bussey's sister had slipped a quartet of Thai sticks through the mail) and, during the process, started talking to our waiter in an absentminded way.

"How does the Apartheid system work on you, pal?" Bussey could ask anybody anything, it was a certain kind of pagan charm he had.

"Huh?"

We periscoped the oversized menu to stare at brother Wong; twenty years old and obviously active on the hormonal-masturbation level. Bussey spontaneously decided to make a run at the young dude's head, there were only three other customers in the place, no fast movements needed.

"I was just curious to know something about how a young Chinese dude deals with segregation, Apartheid, American style."

"You wanna try duh chicken chow mein, it's good."

"Sounds okay, but I was askin' you a question, young sir?" Brother Wong was obviously feeling uncomfortable about questions that had nothing to do with the menu.

"Skip it man, the dude obviously doesn't want to answer your question."

28

"But he must, I'm a paying customer." Brother Wong smiled cautiously. We had touched a sensitive chord. "What do you want to eat?" he asked impatiently. Bussey, never one to give up anything, announced in Orson Welles type tones.

"We'll have three orders of Chicken Chow Mein, as you suggested, and four beers. You have Chinese beer, Tin Ding, don't you?" The waiter nodded yes. "And an answer to my questions."

"What question?"

"I asked you, pure 'n simple as dog shit, how does this segregation down here affect you?"

"We are not segregated. Your order will be ready in a few minutes."

Wongs...

Simone danced around the large, red-rimmed room. The small Chinese castles, painted red and trimmed in gold hanging over us in the dim light made for a nice touch. Too bad about the food.

"How long you think this place has been here?"

"Well, it was here when I was a girl, I know that for certain."

How do you ask a woman how old she is, if she looks twenty-five and has four children? "I'm forty-five and you know the food is quite oily here."

"I've eaten here before, I have an idea what it's like."

We exchanged coded smiles.

The noodles has been fried, for a long time, in lard, probably. The chicken, too, and the egg rolls, but it tasted good, somehow. I stared at her from time to time, fascinated by the beauty of the woman in front of me. She was incredibly gracious. She nodded to people in other booths, she spoke to babies as they toddled by, she greeted old friends. Of course, this was her turf, she grew up there. I

29

was beginning to get a mental fix on where Leon was coming from.

"Now then, we've had our greasy Chinese food. Tell me what Leon wants to have you say?" She talked like a quirky writer, one of those people who had invented a style all their own. And charmed you with just the hint of a forty-five year old virgin behind it.

'Yeahhhh, I think she's a virgin.'

'But I thought you said she has four kids?'

'She does, but she hasn't been touched. She talks about her husband as though they used to make love through a hole in a blanket. Or maybe a sheet on warm nights.'

'I don't think she's ever had anybody go straight to the center of her bein.'

'And you think you're the man to do it?'

They made a good match, Leon and Simone, I could see them going off somewhere, being happy. I wanted to help them, they were special people to me.

"How can I begin this? We talked for hours about you, about the times we, you all have spent together and what it all meant."

"What did it mean?" Her eyes actually sparkled as she lowered her head for the charge. I felt like I was in over my head. How could this brother have gotten me into a situation like this?

"It meant spending a misty Sunday morning, strolling on the south side of the lake, watching the swans, not saying anything."

She withdrew the intended charge and settled back into the booth. "I've been told that they have an excellent cocktail. Why don't you have yourself one? I don't imbibe myself."

"I don't imbibe..."

She was so funny. Some of it seemed almost deliberate.

The eccentric librarian. And it was all cut short when it was time to be serious. The martini was dry, the olive succulent. Leon would approve. Strange ass place, they couldn't get fried rice right, but they could do a martini. I suddenly felt warm, loose. Was the spirit of Leon entering my being?

"Here's looking at you, kid."

"That sounds like a quotation from something. What is it?"

Was she joking? Everybody knew that line. "It's what Bogart says to Ingrid Bergman, in *Casablanca*."

"Oh." Her face went into suspended animation for a moment, the woman changed moods fast.

"You mean, you've never seen *Casablanca*?"

"If it was a novel, I would've read it, but if you're talking about movies, I haven't been to one since I was a girl."

Yes, the spirit of Leon was infusing my being. I felt sorry for her. How could you not go to a movie? They were like food and water. "May I ask why?"

"What if I refuse to say why? Will it matter that much to you?"

I drained my martini and signalled for another. She could force you into the truth zone so fast it was bewildering. She was serious. If you wanted to rap with her, you had too be about something. Her focus was on being up front, she could smile, laugh and be serious all at the same time.

"Leon is always saying that whatever matters to one person should matter to all people."

"Are you quoting the great man, or reading from an engraved stone?"

"I guess that does sound pretentious, to be quoting a friend of mine."

"I guess it's alright if what's being said is true, or been found to be true over the ages." She said it with a smile and meant every word. "But we're going away from the reason

31

you chose to surrender your Saturday afternoon to someone else's lady friend." The corners of her mouth crinkled. I was beginning to feel that Leon had sacrificed me because he needed a rest. The sister was straight up. And the inevitable was approaching. He had given me a list.

"I'd like to stay on what matters, and what doesn't matter for just a little bit."

She turned her head slightly to one side, looking out of the corners of her eyes. "I don't think what matters has to necessarily be tested by truth or time. What matters is determined by the person who says or thinks that it matters.

"In a sense, it matters because I think. I think it matters. Now then, to get back to the reason why I chose to 'surrender' my Saturday afternoon to someone else's lady friend." She looked pleased with me. Almost the kind of angelic-patronizing look your proud schoolteacher laid on you back in the first grade."

"Yes, I'm very interested in hearing this."

I sipped my martini for strength and decided to tell her the truth. "Leon is in love with you, but like a lot of younger men, his hormonal stuff gets in the way of him moving on the real deal."

"I can't but notice that you're also a younger man, Herb. What gives you the insight to say what you're saying? Do you know what the real deal is? Sounds like she's trying to trick me into saying something I can't defend."

"Yes, I think I do. It's what matters to me, that's the real deal."

"And this thing about his 'hormonal stuff,' what's that mean?" We locked eyeballs. Was I going to chicken out?

"Leon wants to make love to you."

"Did he tell you to tell me that?"

The gin in the glass was so smooth, I hardly felt like I was swallowing anything. "He didn't tell me to come right

32

out and say that but he has expressed the desire, yes."

"What did he say?" She stared down into her tea cup, nostrils flaring slightly, cheeks blazing. At that moment, she looked like the sexiest woman in the country.

"Which version do you want to hear?"

"How many are there?"

"Only two. The official version that he gives me, laying on his bunk with his head cradled in his hands. And the unofficial version that I see swimming in his eyes."

"That's the version I want to hear."

I got the unmistakable feeling that she had placed her hand in my lap, that it was just resting on the length of my penis. She hadn't, of course, it was just the heat of the question. "Are you sure?"

"What's wrong, don't you think I'm old enough to listen to unsanctioned language?" She looked hurt, as though tears were welling up in her eyes. 'You've got to remember, man, on the emotional side, she's still a little girl. Her husband kept her pregnant from the time she was sixteen until she was twenty five and in between times, she was only a wife. You understand what I'm saying, Herb, she's only been somebody's wife and mother.'

'She ain't never been nobody's mistress, the "other woman," a "loose woman," none of that. I got to talkin' with her one afternoon, about what it was like, sexually, groin' up on the streets of Chicago and I thought she was going to cum, just listening to me.'

"I didn't mean to indicate, in any way, that you weren't allowed to hear what he said. It's just that, well, I'm just giving you an interpretation. It might not be right."

She nodded.

"I've been reading long enough to know how to read between lines." The waiter placed another discreet martini in front of me. Did she signal for it?

"He wants to crawl up between your legs and just do it to you, on one level. You understand what I'm saying'?'' She nodded quietly, staring straight into my mouth. "That's what his physical urge is about. I can see his dick...his penis gets hard every time he talks about you."

"And this gives you the indication that he wants to 'crawl up between my legs'?"

"Yes, but that is not the only sign." She fed me bait with her eyelashes, the flicker of her tongue into the corners of her lips. I suddenly flashed to what some anthropologist called the imitation vaginal lips. Her lipstick seemed to glow. "Sometimes, when he talks about holding you, in his arms, naked..." I paused to enjoy the impact I was making. "He squirms around, sort of like a person trying to dance, layin' flat on his back."

"And after he has crawled up between my legs and had his way with me, then what?!" She sounded angry.

"See what I mean? I wanted you to know how he really feels and that angers you."

"No, it doesn't. I just want to know what I get out of it." A shrewd smile jarred me. Was she pulling my leg?

"Simone, I'm talkin' about big time lovemaking." The Wong's didn't seem to care how long we stayed, as long as we ordered something from time to time. It didn't seem that we had been there two hours.

"Yes, I gather that you're talking about big time lovemaking. You're using all the proper words."

"Look, don't you understand? Nothing is happenin' for the man who enjoys making love, if nothing happens for the woman."

"I don't see how that's so, after all, it's a rare man who can't use a woman to deposit his sperm into."

Bussey, our resident philosopher had a name for them, he called them "damaged divas." I don't know if Simone fit the total picture of a "damaged diva," but it was obvious that she had not had a sensitive lover in her life. Score one for Leon.

"Hmmmmm..., that's a unique way to look at it."

"What's unique about it? Men have been using women like seminal spittoons for ages."

"Pardon me for differing with you, but that is not true." I could almost visualize her rolling up her imaginary sleeves, getting ready to do battle. She obviously loved a good argument.

"I hope you can offer me some convincing proof."

"I don't know how convincing it'll be, but I hope you're open to another point of view."

"Try me."

I suddenly felt tired of the whole business. What purpose would it serve to convince her of anything? If I talked myself blue in the face, what good would it do? Muntuna's beautiful vacant smile flashed through my head.

"You seem to be hesitant about trying to back up your claim about men."

"I'm not hesitant. I was just thinking about the best way to approach this." Brother Wong tipped over with a fresh pot of tea. She sipped and I sipped. "Look, let's face it. Some men have been and always will be dogs, okay? There's nothing we can do about them, in the same way that some women have their defects, too. What I'm talking about, the men that I'm trying to make a case for are not cut from common cloth. We're talking about men who consider themselves lovers." I took note of the way her eyes flashed when she heard the word love. Or sex. Or friends. "Men who are lovers wouldn't think of simply using a woman as a seminal spittoon, it's just not a part of their psychological make up, Simone..." I was actually beginning to feel like Leon. How to explain the beauty and sensitivity of the love

35

act to a woman who had not come close to having that?

"Yes?"

"Let me put it to you this way. Love and loving is an exchange. We give each other something. Let's say, if you, the woman, simply decided to give me...uhh, have sex with me and that's all you were giving me, I would be disappointed."

She frowned. "I find that hard to believe. It seems to me, from all I've ever read about it, that the only thing men want is what they want and that's it!" She sounded almost bitter, but there was still that glint of humor in the corners of her eyes.

"Let's stay on the track, please. I'm not talking about the sexual con artists. I'm talking about men who consider themselves serious lovers. Serious lovers want to go beneath the surface, get into the core of things. It's very difficult to...beg pardon my French, fuck and make love at the same time." She glared at me for a moment.

"What's the difference?"

"The difference?"

"Between fucking and making love?" I doubt if her mouth had ever formed the word, except on the printed page of a book. Her face, even in the dim Wong lighted room, shaded into reddish. Well, Leon had warned me what I was in for, but he hadn't prepared me. How could he?

"We have to be very frank about this."

"Of course."

"Awright, now then. We got two people fuckin', okay?" She took a sip of her tea and nodded me on. "One thang you got to understand is that fuckin' is delicious, it's like fudge sundaes, cold coca-colas on a hot day, almost anything your sense can come to grips with that makes you feel orgasmic. Dig?" She was swaying in time to my rhetoric. I felt like I was making progress. "Two people are in it for the nut value, that's fuckin'. All that's ever going to come out of their relationship is a nut. Now, please don't misunderstand me. A nut can be really nice, if that's how deep you are." I don't know, maybe it was my imagination, or the Wong martinis, but it seemed that she was really smiling at me, without any malice of thought, for the very first time. "That's right, if all they're interested in is the nut, well, that it's fairly easy to come to."

"For the man, you mean." Leon had been straight out about what he knew. Or thought. 'I don't think the woman has ever had an orgasm, man. I don't think she'd recognize one if it bit her.' I had to operate from that premise.

"Yes, Simone, of course, it's a given that most men will have an orgasm, if they can have an erection, but that doesn't necessarily deny the woman an opportunity to have an orgasm, too."

"That sounds like, if it's good, it's supposed to cause good to happen."

I signaled for another martini. Shit! If we were going to dive all the way down into it, why not get loose? The Wong family cast eyes out at us from very conceivable crevice. Brother Wong paraded the martini over on a tiny silver tray. Had they used that one before?

"Yeahhh, yes, Simone, you got that basically correct. If the things that had messed the Anglo-Saxon Western White man up is that he thought that lovemakin' and sex and all of that, was nasty."

"Whooaa, just a minute, my friend, aren't you gettin' off the track here?" I was beginning to love her sense of dialectics. Damn! How often could you rap to a sister who knew her stuff?

"I don't think so."

"I do. What's the point of bringing the 'Anglo-Saxon Western White man into what we're talking about?"

"As much as I hate to say it, and I really mean that, as much as I hate to say it, the Anglo-Saxon-Western White man and the Southern European White man, let's color them Spanish/Portuguese, and a whole bunch of other weirdos, including Freud, have fucked around in our lives . . ."

"Do you mean that in the sense of fuckin' that you defined a while ago?"

Clever lady. She forced me to think back to what I had said. Part of it had to be true, in relation to the master-slave relationship that the Anglo-Saxon Protestant sexual code had been applied to me.

"Simone, you gotta think it out. First, we have to go to where we had it. We can't begin to deal with our African-American love/sex lives as though it all started happening when the Portuguese picked up on us. You've read enough Black history to know that the story of Africans didn't begin with the creation of African history, from the European point of view." I wanted to lean over and kiss the lady flush on the mouth. She inspired that kind of feeling, just from the way she listened to what I was saying. I wasn't certain that she was in total agreement with what I was saying, but she was listening. Was I right? I signalled for another martini. Was it my fourth? Fifth?

"I don't know if this is the truth or not but my intuition forces me to say that we had a better loving life before the European showed up. We didn't have indecision, men were men and women were women, and there were avenues for people of the same sex who dug each other to explore. But few did because, before the European cult of Narcissism plowed in, we seemed to be very comfortable with heterosexuality. Men were forced to please women, on the African level, because there were built in controls to guarantee that. You couldn't just simply fuck, if you can dig where I'm coming from?"

38

She nodded politely, neutrally, listening carefully.

"Like, I mean, there were people who were 'specially designated to talk about your ass, if you didn't take care of business." I was startled to hear her laugh out loud. Wowwww! "What I'm tryin' to get into, is a story that's Our story, that became His-story and is about to become Our-story again. And it's got something to do with love/sex/romance, all of it."

The restaurant was no longer a place where food was served. It was where we came to discover truth and explore honesty. And I was going to be the honest teacher. "Any time we pay attention to our true selves, anything in this whole round world becomes possible. We were led astray, soulfully, psychologically, physically, some of us.

"Now, those are the dogs, those are the brothers who've been led so far astray by 'foreign' ideas and programming that they don't really see women in their true light. As a matter of fact, there are men, if you want to call them that, who habitually refer to women as bitches. That's how far off they've gotten from the track."

"So you're saying that the Black men who can ignore the ravages of slavery are great lovers."

I was ready for her. She wanted to play hardball. "No, not at all. The point I was trying to make is that there's an immense difference between men who want to love and men who want to simply fuck. I'd be willing to bet you that you probably could tell what the difference is by listening to the way different men talk; men who are simply fuckers use words like 'bitch' and 'motherfucker' a lot."

"And the other types?"

"Well, we say 'baby,' 'honey,' 'sweetheart,' 'lady,' 'sister' and a few other things, a lot."

Momma Wong eased the bill onto the table beside my left elbow. "Y'all come back'n see us again, you heah?" She

39

said quietly and eased away. Simone smiled at the woman's back and flashed an even bigger smile at me.

"Well, Leon-Herb, or should I call you Herb-Leon?"

"You can't go wrong, either way."

"I must say...you've certainly been informative. I have to say that I've learned some new words even. I can't honestly say that I completely agree with everything you've said, but it's been interesting."

The bill 'corrupted' $24.45 of my hard earned money. "You know, I really feel that we should go dutch on this," she suggested.

"I wouldn't think of it; please, dear lady, cease and desist from making remarks of that nature."

She liked that, I could tell. It probably had to do with all of the English novels she'd read. We made a slow, royal exit. She had a beautiful body. Every male eye in the late afternoon dinner crowd agreed with me. I felt slightly buzzed and quite pleased with myself. I made a quick replay of the mental tape as we strolled out into the parking lot. It had come off rather well, I thought. Maybe I had laid it on a bit too thick with the stuff about loving and fucking, but what the hell? How else could you say it?

"Well, how you doin', Mr. Herb?"

I'm sure I must have done the most classical double take of all time. Muntuna, of all people!

"Ohh, Muntuna, what're you doin'...uhhh, I mean, where did you...?"

Her girlfriend flexed her left leg into a relaxed stance and took several excited chomps on her mouthful of gum, prepared to enjoy the scene. Simone crossed her arms on her breast and shot Muntuna a hard look.

"And how're you doing this evenin', Miss Adams?"

Muntuna immediately backed off of her hands-on-hip-pissed-off stance. I was fascinated by the abrupt change.

"Oh, hi Mrs. Williams, hi you doin'?"

"I'm fine...and when are you going to return those two *National Geographic Special* books? We have a number of other people who'd like to read those books."

Muntuna actually looked embarrassed. This was the brassy nineteen year old who didn't "take no stuff from nobody"? the sister who was taking me through changes?

"Uhh, I'm gonna bring them in tomorrow, first thing."

"You better, else I'm gonna have to put a check in front of your name. And how're you doin', Lucille?" The gum chomper paused to say, "fine" and kept on chomping.

"You girls goin' in here to have some of Mr. Wong's special grease?"

"Uhh huh."

"You know how Lucille is when she gets paid. And besides, I didn't have nothing else to do, after I had been stood up."

Muntuna's expressive eyes left no doubt in anybody's mind that I was the villain. I wanted to defend myself but I didn't know how. Simone grabbed hold of the whole scene in a flash. "I find it hard to believe that any man would stand you up, Muntuna."

Muntuna rolled her eyes at me. "Well, it happens sometimes."

Simone shifted without a pause. "I didn't introduce Mr. Herb. My goodness! I don't know your last name."

"It's Carson."

"I didn't introduce Mr. Carson, because I got the feeling that you've already met."

Muntuna went back into her evil woman stance. "We know each other."

"That's good, then you already know what a nice young man he is. We've just had a meeting and Mr. Carson, Herb, and some of the members of his unit have agreed to sponsor the library's youth club. Don't you think that we wonderful of them to do that?''

I'm sure my surprised blinking matched Muntuna's surprised blinking. Was this lady fast on her feet or was she fast on her feet? We nodded in unison. Muntuna was nodding in agreement. I don't know why I was nodding. I took it all in. We had had a meeting alright, and of course, it would be a simple matter to get a few of the brothers to donate some of there 'good time' money to the library's youth club. No problem. What I really liked is the way she did it. In a few sentences and a stern glance she had turned Muntuna's hard head around, forced a measure of respect out of her and spread a little gloss on my persona at the same time. ''Now then, Mr. Carson, can I drop you somewhere?''

One glance at Muntuna's pouting lower lip canceled out any other plans I might've had. ''Uhh, no thanks, Mrs. Williams, I think I'm going to go back in here and take another look at my fortune cookie.''

''Alrighty. You take care now. If you happen to have the chance, drop into the library about the middle of next week and I'll give you all the material you need about the youth club activities. Or would you prefer to have me mail it?''

''I'll pick it up, no problem.''

''Give my regards to the other members of your unit.''

''Sure will.''

Muntuna had threaded her arm around mine and was whispering fiercely into my ear. ''You, jive turkey! Why didn't you tell me that you was meeting with Mrs. Williams? Did you think I was goin' to be jealous or something?''

I decided to play it out. ''Well after all, she is a woman and you know how you women can be about each other.'' I turned to catch Simone's conspiratorial wave and wink. God, what a fine woman. Muntuna pursed her lips into an annoyed pucker.

42

"Why should I be jealous of a woman that old? She went to high school with my mother. Anyway, that's a nice thing you guys are doin'. I bet Leon probably thought it up."

Papa Wong showed none of the surprise that the rest of the people in the restaurant showed as I re-entered with Muntuna and her girlfriend, Lucille. "Afternoon, hi'yall this hot afternoon?" He shuffled the oversized menu's out to us and stood to one side with his pen and pad at port arms. I didn't have to study the menu, I knew what the speciality of the house was.

"I'll have a dry martini."

"And the young lady?"

"They'll have to think it over for a bit. Give'em a few minutes." I sipped my martini, feeling suave and quite sophisticated, listening to Muntuna and Lucille make decisions, change their minds, decide on something else and change their minds again. They were such beautiful young fluffy heads. I studied them as they zigzagged and stutter stepped through the menu. Lucille, at eighteen? Nineteen?, was already beginning to have that 'heavy set' look. I'd never seen her when she didn't have something in her mouth or was about to put something in her mouth. Leon joked about her. "If that chick likes to do it as much as she likes to eat, somebody out there is gon' have a terrible hurtin' put on 'em."

Muntuna Adams, built in the classic African mold, slender hips with a cute lil' bumble bee body, slender calves and gorgeously formed thighs. Her biggest concerns seemed to be lipstick shades, nail polish and hairdos. "Herb, what're you gonna have 'side from that martini or whatever it is you got?"

"I'd like to have you, that's what I'd like to have."

Lucille peeled off another stick of gum into her mouth and raised the menu to cover the dirty smirk on her face. Muntuna

43

lowered her eyelids and rimmed her ruby dark lips with her tongue. The look was either a promise or a threat. I couldn't tell which.

In any case, I was prepared.

Chapter 4

I didn't make it back to the post 'til 2:00 a.m., but I couldn't stand it anymore. I had been teased into almost a comatose state by Muntuna's indecision.

"Herb, do you know that I'm practically a virgin?"

"No, I didn't know that."

"Well, you know it now."

After a couple more martinis for me and some greasy chop suey for Muntuna and Lucille, we had (I should say) managed to make Lucille feel unwelcome enough to find something else to do.

"Why don't you just come right out and say that you don't want me hangin' out with y'all?"

"Lucille, I don't want you hangin' out with . . ."

"Awww c'mon, Herb, don't be so cruel!"

"That' awright, Munnie, he ain't hurt my feelin's none. I got lotsa stuff to do. I'll call you tomorrow. Good bye, Herbert!"

Strange, as soon as friend Lucille turned the corner, Muntuna's whole scene changed. "Herb, my folks went over to South Carolina to visit my Aunt Patsy. You wanna come sit on the porch?" We linked our arms around each other and started trolling. That was one of the things that I really loved about Augusta. There was no place that wasn't within walking distance. It would be hard describe how good I felt. I had spent the early afternoon rappin' to a lady on my partner's behalf, and now here I am, in the early evening, strolling with my very own lady. I felt blessed...a little buzzed on the Wong martinis. Tonight was going to be the night, I knew it.

"Herb, why you walkin' so fast?"

"Oh, I didn't realize."

She smiled at me. I loved her smile, it was warm, lush, Southern. We left the lights of the restaurant, the corner drugstore, the Mom 'n Pop store and the gas station behind us and wandered through the neighborhood. Some may have left their hearts in San Francisco, spent their Aprils in Paris, but I'm sure I left my soul in Augusta. The heat of the day had lingered, cooled by the night, into a kind of sensual mood. Fragrances seemed to be milked into the air from every place.

"Mmmmm, what's that?"

"That beautiful odor, like perfume?"

"Oh, that's magnolia, you never smelled magnolia before?"

"Not quite that heavy."

From time to time, on the fragrant dark streets, I would stop, fold her into my arms and give her the most tender kiss I could come up with. Brother Bussey, our resident phraseologists from Bed-Sty, New York, used to say, "You gotta get to 'em by being brutally affectionate, incredibly tender." She would return my kiss as openly and warmly

46

as I gave it and then we'd continue strolling, as though nothing had happened.

"Herb, what're you going to do when you get out of the service?"

She caught me by surprise with her question. She was always catching me by surprise. We were a block away from her house. "Ohhh, I don't really know. Get a job, do what I was doing before I got drafted."

"And what was you doin'?"

I felt tempted to lie, to build myself up into something I'd never been. "Not too much of anything, if you want to know the truth."

"I always want to know the truth," she said, and circled her arms around my waist and squeezed me to her. At that moment she could've been a delicious piece of something. I felt the strong muscles in her back, the gorgeous tenderness of her spirit pressed against me. I felt that I was telling her the truth when I said, "I love you, Muntuna."

She didn't say anything, just opened the gate and led me up onto the porch by my little finger. Old fashioned Southern porch/veranda, with trellises rambling up the sides of the entrance, Gardena bushes flanking the stairs. You could sit on the porch and never be seen by anyone passing by. There was a sofa to sit on.

"Wait here, I'll get us a couple pillows to sit back on." Life was so simple, no one locked their doors and people spoke to each other in the streets. It was an innocent world. Innocent and dangerous. The cracker police were just as apt to shoot you as call you "boy." The Ku Klux Klan was likely to make a swing through and toss a few sticks of dynamite on some "uppidy nigger's" porch, and often did. Or the heat of the summer, coupled to a din of fatalistic urge, would call strong Black men to knife each other in low down, bucket-of-blood joints out on the edge of town. No, all was not

47

romance and inevitable happiness.

She tripped back out with two overstuffed pillows and a small glass. "This is some o' my daddy's corn."

"That's thoughtful of you."

I had met Mr. and Mrs. Adams twice and could hardly remember what they looked like, aside from the fact that the father was very light and the mother very dark. I don't mean to say that they were anonymous faces or anything. They just didn't make an impression on me.

I sipped the two fingers of corn liquor and watched the fireflies for a few minutes. Tonight was definitely going to be The Night. "Muntuna, how long have we known each other?"

"About four months," she spoke with her head leaning back against the sofa, as though she were dreaming.

"And during all that time, have I ever made any kind of demands on you?"

We both edged closer to each other.

"What kinda demands?"

"You know." I gently placed my hand on the inside of her thigh. Her voice trembled a little when she spoke.

"No, I don't guess you have made any demands on me."

The echoes of people laughing, having a good time, drifted past. It was Saturday night in the African sector of 'Gusta. I leaned over and kissed her. I felt like standing her up in front of me and undressing her, piece by piece. "I really care about you, baby, you know that, don't you?"

"Uh huhhh," she moaned. She had taken off her panties, that little rim of cotton circling her thighs was gone.

"What time are you expecting your parents back?" The question was like a splash of ice water on her face. She popped up off the sofa and pulled her skirt down in one motion. "I don't know."

"What time are you expecting them?"

"They could get back any time." The mood had suddenly changed. She seemed almost angry. I sat there, taking little sips on the corn, trying to sort things out. "Did I say something wrong?"

She folded her arms and looked off into the darkness. "No, Herb, you didn't say anything wrong." She held my head between her hands and began to peck little kisses on my eyes, cheeks, lips and ears. I pulled her to me and kissed her, hard. She pulled away slightly. "Herb, you want to make love to me, don't you?"

"Yes, I do."

"And I want you too, I really do. But. . ."

"But what?"

I was prepared to overcome all opposition. You're on your period, no problem. Disease? I have rubbers. Frigid on the edges? I'll unthaw you. What?!

"But what happens then? What happens after I let you make love to me?"

I had the urge to get right up and walk away. I hated that kind of sexism. 'After I let you make love to me?' We had never quite gotten to this point before. "What do you want to happen?"

"Well, if you really wanna know, I'd like to get married and move away from Augusta. That's what I been savin' myself for."

I slumped back on the sofa. Muntuna had won again. "I hadn't thought about getting married. Not yet anyway." What else was there to say? Why not be honest about it? She relaxed against me, squirming around in my lap.

"That's one of the things I really love about you, Herb, you know that? You're honest."

The emotional heat shot back up again. She was fire and ice and I loved every moment of it for some perverse reason. She suddenly sprawled back on the sofa as though everything

49

she'd just said was forgotten. "Lay on top of me, Herb. Kiss me again. I love for you to kiss me."

Fifteen minutes later, just at the point when she was going to decide whether we should go in the house, to her bedroom, or get stark ravin' naked on the front porch, Mr. and Mrs. Adams rattled up in a car that seemed to run on backfires and smoke. I guess I should've been grateful to them for relieving the awful tension. Were we, or weren't we? I gave them a respectful, "Evenin', Mr. and Mrs. Adams" as they entered and they returned the greeting twofold.

"Evenin', son. Evenin', son."

Like I said, I didn't get back to the post 'til 2:00 a.m., feeling like I had been taken through a sexual wringer. Leon sprang up into a sitting position on his bunk as soon as he saw me stroll up the aisle of the barracks. If ever a person's body language spoke of anxiety...

"Well?" he asked.

"Well what?" I responded, feeling no need to jump the gun on anything.

Muntuna had promised me that next week would be different.

'Next week will be different, you'll see.'

"Well, what happened?"

I put the brother on hold 'til after I took a quick shower. Fortunately, we had the barracks to ourselves, except for PFC Woodrum, the good ol' boy from 'West by Gawd Virgina,' who was sleeping off another Saturday binge.

"Okay, now then, brother man. What was it you wanted to know?"

Leon was so serious about the situation, it wasn't even possible to joke with him about it. "Start at the beginning, and don't leave anything out."

I started at the beginning and I didn't leave anything out. He was smiling his ass off by the time I'd finished. "Herb, you don't know what this means to me, man."

I thought about asking him to go to bat for me with Muntuna, but the irony of it prevented me from making the proposal. We leaned over and shook hands before calling it a night.

"Leon, I have some idea what it means to have your nose open, believe me."

Chapter 5

Leon was catching hell from Sergeant Shearing. We all knew it and we could all see it, even on Sunday.

"Leon, what the fuck are you doing, man?"

"What's it look like I'm doing, I'm changing into fatigues so that I can clean up under the barracks."

"Clean up under the barracks? On Sunday?"

"It was asshole Shearing's idea."

The Quintet (Bussey, McKinnon, Steel, Dalomba and myself) put our spiritual arms around the brother. That was all we could do to let him know that he wasn't in this alone. The situation could've been funny if it had been on television maybe. What did we have to deal with? An ol' fashioned cracker sergeant who had to curl his mouth into all kinds of weird shapes just to prevent himself from saying 'Nigra.'

"We'll have ever'body, ever swingin' horn in this unit to understand one dangblasted thang. And that is that we do not practice dis-crimination in this good Army." If any

Nigra..."

"That's 'knee-gro,' Sergeant Shearing."

"If any knee-gro soldier reports to me that he feels that he's been discriminated against, in any way, shape, form or fashion, action will be taken immediately, if not sooner."

That was the official non-discrimination speech he was required to make every other month. We laughed ourselves silly afterwards and maintained our guard. There were six and a half of us in a 120 man unit (the 'half' was a dude from Brazil who couldn't figure out what he was when it suited his purposes. He looked like a regulation brother to me, even with his curly hair) and the sergeant's 'non-discrimination' speech didn't mean shit. The town surrounding the post was labeled 'colored' and 'white.' The condition of the part of the world we were in was totally segregated and we were supposed to believe that some kind of action was going to be taken if one of us complained of discrimination? It was all a big joke. The job was going to be on the one, or ones, who 'dis-criminated' against us. We couldn't do much more than write letters to our congressmen about the stuff that trickled down on us from higher up, but the individuals who cracked 'nigger' jokes and acted out of pocket, were made to suffer immediately for their indiscretions.

Bussey laid two black eyes on a white boy from Coker, Alabama who insisted on telling him that 'his nigras' knew their place. I think the problems started for Leon when he was caught writing poetry one day when he was supposed to be on some shit detail or other. Sergeant Shearing confiscated the poem. Leon appealed to the unit commander and Shearing was forced to return the poetry. Things were never the same after that. Don't get me wrong. Life had never been perfect for any of us around Shearing. We had casually labeled him the bigot he was and avoided him whenever

53

possible. In some ways, Leon was made the scapegoat. It wasn't really personal, any of us would have served the purpose. Leon didn't help his case a lot by being the kind of dude he was. The brother wouldn't take any crap from anybody.

"I don't care if they throw me in jail for a hundred years'n a day, I ain't never going to kiss that cracker's ass."

"Ain't nobody askin' you to do that, brother, it just doesn't seem to make a lotta sense to stay on a collision course with this asshole. You know you got guaranteed conflict doin' that."

"Well, let *him* back off then."

Sergeant Shearing didn't back off, of course, not with all the regulations he could call on and Leon, well, Leon just kept on being Leon.

Smith, the company clerk, told me one day, "You know, I think Leon Cole has set a record for having his weekend passes withdrawn." When he did manage to make it to town, he'd come back looking very calm and mellowed out. "We drove to this lake, took a lil' lunch. I picked up a bottle of wine and we sat and talked all afternoon. What's happenin' with you and Miss 'Tuna?"

I was tempted to lie and say that we had gotten into big time lovemaking, but it would've been a lie. Muntuna was doing some incredible things with my head. We had come close to getting it together on the porch a couple more times but someone or something always interfered. I was still praying, hoping and groping. "What's it feel like being out with an older woman?"

He stared at me as though I had a tail. "What do you think? You were out with her one afternoon, how did it feel?"

"That was different, we were having a meeting, remember?"

The brother's eyes would get all milky and shiny when

he talked about Simone. They were into something very interesting. "The first thing you have to remember about Simone, Herb, is that she's one of these special people in the world. It doesn't have a lot to do with the fact that she's a woman. Or a certain age. To be frank with you, I find it hard to attach any age to who she is. You know what I mean?"

"Awww c'mon, man, age might not be the biggest obstacle in the way of y'all gettin' it all together, but as I recall you were tryin' to open her head up to some other things. What's happenin'?"

I was dying to hear about their love life, but I tried to be casual about it. At that point in time, a vicarious thrill would've done me all the good in the world.

"We kissed for the first time this past Sunday."

I was stunned. How long had he known this woman? Six, seven months? Their first kiss? "C'mon, Leon, you can lay the truth on me. It won't go no further than right here." Their first kiss? Me and Muntuna had gotten into kissing the second hour after we met.

"C'mon, let's walk over to the canteen. I'll pop for a can of that awful beer. Who in the hell ever thought of 3.2 beer anyway?"

"You gonna talk about the kiss?"

"Yeahhh, I'll give your nasty little mind something to feed on." I like Leon. Everybody did, except Sergeant Shearing. It was after chow and the soldiers who lived on post had nothing better to do than roam around. They wandered in and out of the service clubs, in and out of the post theaters, in and out of the canteens.

"Man, I'd kill myself if I had to live the rest of my life like this."

"I'm inclined to agree with you." Maybe it had something to do with the fact that we were slightly older, at twenty-four and Leon's twenty-five, than the average recruit, eighteen, nineteen years old, that made a difference. They just seemed silly as hell to us, especially the gung-ho types.

"Who are these Chinese dudes strolling around here holding hands?"

"That's some weird cultural shit, huh? Actually, they're South Vietnamese, they're goin' to the Signal Corps school."

"South Vietnamese? Where's that?"

"Somewhere in Southeast Asia."

It was 1962, 1964, remember? There was a lot we didn't know then.

We bellied up to the canteen counter.

"Why don't we get about eight of these? It takes three of them for me to get any kind of buzz."

The brassy noise of teenagers away from home for the first time, buoyed by semi-alcoholic beer, forced us back out into the post streets with our brews. "I know a good place to do this."

We wound up sprawled on the P.T. platform behind our barracks. Someone was practicing taps on his trumpet. Somebody else was singing a country and western song. The night air buzzed with the sound of men preparing for war. Or an inspection. We popped open the cans and gulped. We had discovered that it wasn't the kind of beer you could sip.

"Burp! This is some gassy shit, you know?"

"I heard that. Burrp! So, y'all kissed for the first time, huh?"

He settled back on his right elbow, beer can cradled in his left hand. "Yeahhh, we kissed for the first time and it was a terribly disappointing experience for me in some ways."

I spilled beer down my chin. How could any kiss be disappointing with the kind of lips that woman had?

"I have to tell you the truth, man. The sister didn't know

56

a lot about kissing. Don't get me wrong, now. Just accomplishing that much made me feel that we had done something. The kiss made me feel like I was on the verge of something delicious, you know what I mean?"

I couldn't help thinking of the contrast between what he was describing and what kissing Muntuna was like. Her lips and tongue were enough to keep me awake any night.

"Check it out. When the moment came she sorta pursed her lips out and leaned toward me. To tell the truth, I didn't know what to do for a minute. I leaned into her lips with all the 'brutal affection' I could muster...remember the great Bussey's words?"

"Oh, yes!"

We clinked beer cans together.

"I tried, very gently, mind you, to push my tongue between her lips. Nothing happenin'. I went into a head swivel, you know, the way they do in the soap operas? And finally, I opened my eyes to her eyes, staring me point blank in the face. She started crying. 'I guess I'm not too exciting for you, huh? A middle-aged woman who doesn't even know how to kiss.' I cooled her out, I hugged and squeezed her. I told her that kissing was something you had to learn."

"And you were willing to teach her, huh?"

We popped open a couple more cans. "Uhhh, Leon, I know this is kinda personal, but do you think the rest of her, you know what I mean, is like that?"

"We haven't finished with the kiss part yet. I didn't have to tell her that I was willing to teach her, I just got right off into it. We were up at the lake, beautiful day, not too hot, not too humid. I had her lay back and close her eyes. 'Just relax, Simone, think about how warm and beautiful it is today.'"

"A little hypnotism, huh?"

He ignored my comment and talked on hypnotically.

"'Now, Simone, I'm going to ask you to do something that no man has ever asked you to do.'" I could easily visualize the scene; this beautiful woman laying out on a picnic basket, a lovely sacrifice. "She nodded okay, that she was in agreement with what I was going to ask her to do. 'Simone, I want you to uncross your legs and place your hands, palms down, beside your hips."

"Herb, I ain't gonna lie to you, partner. When I took a hard look at this fine sister sprawled out there like that I wanted to crawl on top of her and just start fuckin' like a love-starved Congolese gorilla. But since you had told her the difference between the fuckers and the lovers, I couldn't do nothing crazy."

We drained our cans and simultaneously opened fresh ones. "I heard that."

"She's layin' just the way I asked her, while I'm trying to figure out what to do next. It came to me from out of the blue. 'Simone, I want you to open your legs just a tiny bit more'"

"Did she? Did she do it?"

"Cool it, man. This is my story. Yes, she did. Now, I told her, 'I want you to imagine that something very warm, very hard and delicious is slipping inside of you. It doesn't hurt, there is no pain, and it makes you feel so good you want to...it makes you feel very, very good. You know that lil' shiver she has when something turns her on?"

I nodded 'yes'.. How could I forget it?

"That little shiver came over her. 'Now, Simone, I want you to open your mouth just a little bit, like you were sucking a grape into your mouth. I want you to use your tongue to play around with the grape.' While she was pretending to play around with this imaginary grape in her mouth, I leaned over and shot about an inch of tongue into her mouth and at the same time I placed my right hand right on top of her

58

pussy. I didn't try no finger business or nothing. I just let my hand rest there while I kissed her. The thing about playing with a grape in her mouth must've really struck a chord. She started moaning and sucking on my tongue and squirming around under my hand and shivering like she was really cold."

He paused to take a long pull on his beer as I waited impatiently for him to add the finishing touch. "And then what happened?"

"That's it. I pulled her up into a sitting position and told her, in a 'brutally affectionate' way, that she was now an A-1 class kisser and that she was qualified to kiss me any time she wanted to."

"Leon, I got to give it to you. You really know how to con a lady."

"Herb, I'm not conning this lady. If I had simply been into a con game I would've given up on this sister a while back. You ever hear the expression, 'You can't cheat an honest man'?"

"Yeah, everybody knows that."

"Well, I thing that goes double for women."

"I'm a little bit at sea, man. Maybe it's the beer. What are you after with this woman?"

He took a pull on his can and stared up at the stars for a long moment. "It's semi-mystical, Herb, hard to explain. It may have something to do with where we come from; her, from this well-mannered, genteel life in 'duh Souf' and me from 'dem mean streets in Chitown'. Like, I mean, I never would've met a woman of her class comin' from where I come from. And vice versa. Sometimes, when I'm with her I feel like a beast, and I feel that she's taming me, somehow."

"I can relate to that, but it still doesn't explain what the real deal is with you and her."

"Like I said, it's semi-mystical. Sometimes I feel like I've

59

known her in another life."

It was my turn to stare at the stars for a bit. My situation wasn't quite that complex. Me and Muntuna were scheduled to get into a heavy dose of physical drama and that was probably all there was going to be to it. "You see yourself being married to her?"

"We got married last week."

"What? Why didn't you tell the gang?! We would've given you all a reception or something."

"We got married when we kissed. What we have to do now is figure a way to be together 'til death do us part."

"Is the kiss like a consummation of the marriage?"

"No, it isn't, Filthy McNasty. The consummation will happen when it's time."

"I envy, you, brother. I really do."

"Why?"

"How many of us are privileged to know something about the kind of love you have?"

"Not many, thank God. I would hate for special relationships to become common. Hey, we better get on in and get ready for tomorrow's happy horseshit."

We hopped down off the P.T. stand and took a couple of wordless pisses. I stumbled across the P.T. field, thinking about Muntuna.

60

Chapter 6

It was January and we were on the verge of spending our first real winter in Georgia. Brother Steel had called a meeting of the 'Seven Musketeers' to talk about a serious problem.

"As you all probably know by now, 'Asshole' Shearing has forced our friend, Leon, into becoming a fireman. As I understand it he gave him no choice. It was either become a fireman, or spend some time in the stockade."

The fireman's job was the lowest end of all sticks. Firemen (they usually had two) shovelled coal into the furnaces that heated up the nine buildings on our company street. It was a filthy job, shoveling coal, and it was usually reserved for deadbeats. The deal was to work twenty-four on and twenty-four off. The kind of working hours that no one in the private sector would ever consider. Twenty-four hours on and twenty-four hours off? That was the way it was. and if you were caught goofing off during your twenty-four hour 'on' period, you were eligible to do some time in the stockade. Like I said, it was a deadbeat's detail.

Brother Bussey came up with a suggestion that was seriously considered for a while. "I think we ought to take Shearing out. You know what I mean? I think we oughta just gon'on 'n take him out. Look, we're all draftees. We're gonna be out of this shit in a few months. Just think of the favor we would be doing future generations of draftees who're going to come in here and suffer under the Asshole."

Maxwell ("I'm from 'ELA,' on the Coast"), thought that Bussey's idea had some merit but he was concerned about the effect it would have on Leon. "I mean, you know the first person they're gonna jack up is Leon. I'm for making a hit on Asshole but I also think it would be counterproductive."

Da Loma and McKinnon had mixed feelings. One was for a petition and the other wanted to do a documentary film on the situation.

Leon popped in, a big smile on his face. "You dudes must be out of your minds. What makes y'all think some injustice is being done to me?"

"I mean, don't get me wrong, I appreciate your concern, but has anybody ever thought about how much the fireman's detail gets you out of? You walk around in dirty fatigues for twenty-four hours, with a shovel on your shoulder, shoes not shined, belt buckle unpolished. You don't have to make formations and you're damned near your own boss because no one gives a damn about you, unless you let the fires go out."

It didn't go quite that smoothly, but a few months later, McKinnon decided to become a fireman, too. He liked the anti-military flavor of the fireman's job. The only problem was that Shearing kept on Leon's ass. In addition to working twenty-four hours, he would sometimes be required to make formations. And even inspections. If you can imagine how hard it was to get ready for an inspection, ordinarily, then you can imagine how hard it was to get ready for an inspection after shoveling coal all night. They worked the brother's ass off, but he seemed to thrive on his twenty-four hours off. When and if they didn't hold him back because his relief hadn't shown up, or put some other kind of stuff in the game. They were trying to break him because they feared him. He was the best soldier in the unit, but the most unmilitary.

He would stand up at unit meetings and say things like, "If I were captured, I wouldn't have to be tortured to tell everything I know. Torture hurts, why endure something like that if you can avoid it?" He stayed angry all the time he was on the post. And, if you saw him off the post he looked angelic. He was giving Simone more kissing lessons. And going through hell.

"Herb, can you see the picture? We're sitting in the car, overlooking this beautiful little harbor and we've been kissing for a half hour. I want to do so much more with her I don't even know how to talk about it.

"I'm meeting her children now. I can get off the bus and walk to her house and we'll sit and talk or go for a ride or something. I don't know what to do. I want to make love to her so bad it actually hurts."

I gave him all the sympathy I could muster but I had problems of my own. Time seemed to be running out suddenly for some of us. Leon kept on shoveling coal.

Muntuna made love to me for the first time that winter, because I promised to marry her. She put me on hold for seconds until I 'got it together.'

The days seemed to drag, filled with insane lectures on how to survive a nuclear war... "Now everything will be fine so long as you remain inside your nuke-proof, all-weather protection garment.''

"But what about food, Sergeant? If the world has been contaminated, won't that affect the food and water?''

What to do when captured by the enemy (most of us felt that we had already been captured by the enemy). We had some draftees who were downright unpatriotic. And finally, we were counting paperclip necklaces that we had hanging in our wall lockers like metal rosaries. 120 clips, 119, 118, 117...

Some people began to experience anxiety attacks 'round about ninety days away from discharge. Jazz sessions at the local joint cooled a few people out. Two a.m. rap sessions helped. Occasional bouts of outright drunkenness, counterbalanced by excessive exercise, occupied one day at a time.

Leon channeled into a gulag. Whenever he had a spare moment, he was with Simone. "She really knows how to kiss now, man, I mean, for real.''

"What's next?''

"I don't really know. I think it's time for us to get into some big time lovemaking now. I really feel that way, but how do I go about it? I'm dealing with a woman who has so little interest in sex.''

"Is she frigid?''

"Noooo! That's the strange part about it. She's really passionate. You can tell that from the way she kisses.''

Leon, I can't believe you can't figure out a way to tell this woman you want to make love to her.''

"Sounds goofy, huh? But dig, check it out. The sister has children old as I am and I'm afraid that she would reject me, if I asked her to make love with me.''

"What does she think the 'kissing lessons' are supposed to lead up to?''

"Nothing. They're just separate things in her head. She doesn't suggest that there's any connection between what we're doing and anything else."

"Is she aware that some people think of kissing as foreplay?"

The brother shrugged. "I don't think she was ever exposed to anything quite that sophisticated. But that doesn't really matter. What I sense is a rare kind of understanding about life and about love, too, but purely on the ethereal side. She reminds me of this Indian woman, a yogini who hasn't eaten in about twenty years." I just stared at him. He was always coming up with stuff like that.

"Hasn't had a bite of anything in the last twenty years, you say?"

"That's correct, my brother. She draws her energy directly from the sun."

"What does she do on cloudy days?"

He didn't crack a smile, or miss a beat. My attempt at humor was being subtly put down. "She fasts on those days."

"Awright, Leon, that's enough. I get the point. So, what's going to happen?"

It would be impossible, at this late date, to try to describe the profound look of sadness that swept across his face. "I don't really know, man, to tell you the absolute truth. I've weighed so many options my head feels like I got a ton of bricks on it. Okay, let me be totally up front about things. Number one, I don't really feel that I can live the rest of my life without this woman. I feel a need for her like you feel a need for food and water. Or beautiful flowers. I broached the idea of getting married to her and you know what she said?"

"I can't imagine."

"She said, 'But Leon, I've already been married,

65

remember?' So, I decided to cool it on the matrimonial number. I thought she would put up an objection about our age difference, her being forty-five and me being twenty-five.

"I'll get back to the marriage part in a bit. What's driving me up the wall now is this celibacy. I'm not adjusting to well to it."

"Leon, are you trying to convince me that you haven't had any for...well, how long has it been?"

"If your memory is long enough, you will recall that we arrived her in April of '62 and I had a little number goin' on with this sweet lil' sister I met when I was hidin' out on post. Her name was Sophronia, or something like that. And that was it. I think I've been waiting for Simone."

"And you're still waiting, but for what?"

He looked off into the distance, his eyeballs glazed with urges. "I'm waiting for Simone to come to me." He was bewildering me.

"Leon, what are you tryin' to do to yourself with this woman?" The question seemed to come from another place. I wasn't sure that I had asked that.

"That's a clever question, Herb, and you're the first one to guess that. I'm using her to purge myself."

Damn, I was really stupid to ask him a question like that. "How can she do it?"

"Just by being herself. She's pure. She can save me from having to ask forgiveness of all the innocent people I've fucked over. Let me give you an example..." You couldn't stop Leon from talking when he really got turned on. "I picked up a young sister one night, on 55th Street, Woodlawn, Jimmy's Tavern, after six, gin 'n tonics. My tongue was so loose in my head I could've lured hummingbirds onto my dick. This young sister, couldn't have been older than fifteen, strolls by, her whole world spread out in front of her.

"I seduced her on the spot, with some bullshit about being an African diplomat's son from somewhere. I didn't feel too bad about it, because a lot of the African brothers were playing the homeland game, too, at the time, in 1958, the sixties, in Chicago. We had a group of Nigerian dudes who were passing women around in a circle. The dude getting on the plane would pass the number on to the incoming member.

"Anyway, I just took the beautiful young Black sister to the park, pulled her panties down and created hair burns." He was making it exciting to listen to. I wondered if I should marry Muntuna.

"I felt like a dog afterwards. I know I got her pregnant. I was socially irresponsible and I felt low. I felt even worse the next time, when I went to pick her up at home, with a load of books under my arm, pretending not to know where 63rd and Cottage Grove Avenue was. Or what they did in the Maryland Hotel . . . when I took her there. I suffered after that evening, having literally raided this gorgeous young black girl's body."

I nodded vigorously. I hadn't heard him rant and rave since he got on the coal detail.

"And I fucked her up! I fucked her up! I took her deepest feelings and manipulated them. I knew that she was self-conscious about being ebony colored, with short kinky hair and this gorgeous African body, man. She looked like one of these beautiful African women that they have on the covers of *National Geographic* magazine, that they look at as a curiosity or something exotic. And we see as fantastic pin-ups. She was like that, man. And I messed her head up. I know I did.

"And I never saw her again, after that night."

"Why should that scene put so much weight on your head?"

"It wasn't only that, it wasn't simply that. It was hundreds of those kinds of times. I used to leave women waiting in my room, start ravin' nekkid in my bed and go to the movies. I caused a lot of emotional hurt to a bunch of people."

"And Simone is going to help you find absolution from all this?"

"Don't be funny, man, we're dealing with some serious psychic problems here. Simone could, if she wanted to, absolve me from all my sins. If I treat her right. The problem I'm having, well, that's the problem, and she clearly understands it. If we sleep together, she'll be just like all the rest. She'll be another body on my census book and that will probably be the end of Simone and Leon. But she's preventing that from happening. She's taking it to another level. She doesn't even relate to where I could be coming from. She doesn't relate to my stuff at all. I'm being forced—pressured to come to a new understanding."

What could I do but nod? I don't know whether it was an understanding nod or a confused nod. He was obviously trying to martyr himself. "So, this new understanding will absolve you from all the rotten shit you've done?"

"Yes, I believe if I do exactly the right thing with this sister, it'll put me in a chosen field, so to speak. Herb, you don't know me very well, man. I used to be the greatest emotional fraud around. It's bad enough when you mistreat someone's feelings, it's a kind of rape that you may never recover from. I have the feeling that Simone has me doing a strange kind of penance."

"Personally, I think you're trying to make a martyr out of yourself."

"It's not that, Herb, nothing like that. I'm trying to cleanse my soul with this woman, that's one of the big things I'm doing."

I knew a few people who thought Leon was really cracked.

68

Sometimes, I thought he was crazy myself. "How is this relationship going to 'cleanse your soul.' I mean, why her?"

"That's the kicker, ain't it? Here we got this beautiful, middle-aged sister with four children who has never really done anything but read books. She is on top of all world events, which new movements are about something and which ones ain't, sees the saber rattlin' shit for what it is, the whole kaduza. But she's emotionally clean. I know that I'm being directed, channeled into her sphere for a deeper reason than bustin' my nuts. And that's where I go back to experiencing supernatural stuff. Don't laugh, okay, Herb?"

"Hey, why should I laugh?"

"Well, you know how it is. Some people might think what I'm going through is funny."

"Let me put your head at ease. I don't think it's funny." He pierced me with one of those strange looks he could lay on you.

"Thanks, Herb, I needed that. You know how it is sometimes, especially with certain brothers. They have a tendency to take everything lightly."

"I'm not taking anything lightly."

"Good. That's good. Me neither. That's why I'm so deeply involved with this woman. I sense that all I have to do is not lie, don't cheat and present myself as a leader of myself, and I'll receive benefits way beyond the norm.

"And Simone has it within her power to grant me all of this, including a sexual experience that's going to cause me to dream about her in future life times."

It was my turn to pierce him with my own strange look.

"You see something that deep happenin', huh?"

"I know it's going to happen."

There was nothing else to add to our conversation. He hung his shovel over his shoulder and marched off to stoke the furnaces. I started trimming my mustache and combing my hair, preparation for a soul session with Muntuna. I hated to admit it, but the sister had laid some heavy drama on me with her number about not giving me any more until I 'got it together.'

Chapter 7

I have to be honest and say that I wasn't particularly attracted to him when he first came into the library. There just seemed to be something too slick about him. I guess you'd call it prejudice, but he didn't give the impression of someone interested in books. It took several visits for me to become convinced that he 'knew his way around the library.'

After the third visit, he started talking to me. And he'd stay until the library closed. It may sound naive, or 'square' as he'd say, but I didn't have the vaguest notion that he called himself courting me. My oldest daughter, Shirley was the one who told me what was happening. "Momma, I think that young soldier comin' in here all the time is kinda sweet on you."

I didn't know whether to be scandalized or amused. It just didn't seem right, somehow for any man to be interested in me. I had only had a relationship with one man and that was

71

Jim. When he died, I just simply assumed that I would be a widow for the rest of my life. It wasn't because men didn't care for me. Such was not the case. I'd received any number of proposals, mostly indecent, from a number of men. I actually had to stop going to church because of that.

I'll never forget the Sunday morning, right there on the front steps after services, when Deacon Jones edged up and whispered, "Miss Williams, last night I dreamed that I had my thang in you."

Leon never made that kind of approach and I'm happy that he didn't. I would've been so hurt and disappointed. The thing about Leon is that I just couldn't see him, I couldn't make the connection between himself and myself. Firstly, he was a year younger than my oldest son. He looked quite mature but he was obviously not as old as I was. And where I come from, which might seem quite old-fashioned, older women only have something to do with older men. Older men, of course, have always had the option to deal with young women, if they chose to do so.

I feel that he might've thought I was behaving in a naive manner, but the truth of the matter is, that I couldn't figure out what he wanted, literally. Yes, I was aware that I was, that I am, an attractive woman. How can you not be aware of it after umpteen people have said, "You're such an attractive woman." In any case, the point I'm trying to make concerns the incongruity of 'us.' He was younger, I was older. And if that wasn't enough of a draw back, he was from a style of life that I could only imagine because I have never experienced it.

When he started talking to me about growing up on the streets of Chicago, it was like listening to a horror story. I guess that's basically where our relationship started, with stories. He'd come into the library and start telling me stories. Some of them were quite charming. He also did an excellent job of interrogating me. It didn't seem that he was doing that, but he was. Quite cleverly, too, I must say.

The first question he asked was whether or not I was married. When I told him that my husband had died of a heart attack he didn't offer condolences. He simply asked me whether or not he had suffered. I liked that.

Firstly, I think he would've been hypocritical to offer condolences; after all he didn't even know the man. He was very patient with me, I must admit. Here is this perfectly well-mannered, rather nice looking young man, coming into the library to see me and everyone seemed to know that was what he was doing, except me. Yes, he was quite patient with me.

One evening, I asked him to help me return the movie projector and screen to the storeroom. He smiled that special little smile of his and when we placed the equipment in the storeroom, he held my face between his hands and kissed me on the lips, very gently. I was thunderstruck. That was the first time. I pretended that it hadn't happened because I didn't know what kind of response to make. The second time, I was a willing participant, but clumsy. He had convinced me that we should spend an afternoon together, take a drive up to Clark Lake on the post and talk. I couldn't see anything wrong with that so I guess you could say we had a date. We had a lovely time and he gave me my first kissing lesson.

There's no need to try to hide my feelings about the matter at this late date. I was beginning to feel that he was a special person in my life but I still didn't know quite where to put him. I think he had basically the same kind of dilemma going on but, being a male animal, he couldn't own up to that. In any case, we had our picnic at the lake and he gave me a lesson in how to kiss. And he touched me, intimately. If it had been anyone else I would've been shocked and disturbed.

73

I somewhat enjoyed this notion he had of me being a guiltless librarian who had learned all about life from reading books. The truth of the matter is, that I had learned quite bit from books but I wasn't completely unaware of what life was all about.

I've always been shy about people, 'specially men. I guess it may have something to do with being married and having a relationship with only one man during the course of my life. Leon worked at pulling me out of my shell, so to speak. And when his sergeant began to give him problems, like withdrawing his weekend passes and such as that, he even sent a friend to spend a few hours with me, to prevent me from 'retreating.' I felt that was terribly considerate of him. His friend, Herb, was almost a facet of Leon. Either that or that they had rehearsed what they were going to say to me so well that when we got together at Wong's Restaurant for lunch (awful food, too greasy)...he sounded like Leon.

We, I could sense that we were heading into deep waters but I felt powerless to stop the drift. Yes, it's true, I needed a man. I wanted a man. My husband had been dead for two years and, despite the fact that we hadn't had the most successful sex life in the world (don't be misled by the fact that we had children), I still felt the urge to have a male. But I wanted more than that. I wanted to share my life with a man. Was Leon going to be that man?

In many ways, I just couldn't see us together. After I fully realized he wanted to make love to me, I'd lay in bed at night and try to figure out where all of this was going to take us. So, he wants to make love to me, I'd think. And what if I let him? What then? One part of me said 'yes, let him do it.' But another part of me, the 'little voice of caution' as my mother called it, whispered 'no.'

He was much younger, he was a soldier and I thought he was just feeling the kind or urge that most men feel when

74

they're away from home. I was also a bit disturbed about our different attitudes toward many things. Leon, for example, was profoundly disrespectful of authority. That was one of the reasons why he wound up shoveling coal. Frankly, I didn't feel too comfortable with his attitude because it gave me the impression that he wasn't well grounded, that he might wind up doing something that would cause him to get in real trouble.

For example, we'd take drives sometimes, to outlaying areas of town, through this beautiful Georgia countryside, where the white folks had even more cracker blood in them than the people in town. Invariably, we'd wind up having problems.

On one occasion, I had to stop Leon from jumping on an old cracker. We had stopped for gas in this little town and this old man shook up a bottle of coca-cola and sprayed it on our windshield. Leon thought he was being insulting or something. I had to explain to him that is was a local custom to do that, to clean off wind shields with coca-cola. He was always on the verge of doing something radical. But it wasn't simply that. We were from different frames of reference. My slow way of doing things, my Southern way, he called it, was a complete contrast to his way of doing things.

We'd have arguments sometimes, very quietly. And when I analyzed the reasons why it would usually go back to our different approaches to things. Leon wanted to assault whatever was bugging him; I wanted to circle around behind it and maybe give it a push out of my life.

Finally, I couldn't get a real sense of who or what he wanted to be in life and I think that disturbed me more than anything else. I knew, if left alone, I would simply wind up being an old maid librarian, but what about him?

I couldn't bring myself to say, "Leon, what're you going to do when you leave here, get out of the Army?" In many ways, it wasn't my business. But never the less, I felt concerned about him. I wanted to help, steer him into some creative area. Why? I don't know. I guess he just seemed to strike me as the rebellious, artistic type. He expressed some interest in writing, but I had a notion that he wasn't serious. That it was simple an overlapping from his love of reading. As a librarian, I was fully acquainted with a host of people who thought they could write because they could read.

All of these kinds of thoughts were constantly going through my mind. And much more. After I had thought myself into a corner, so to speak, I'd always find myself coming back, again and again, to something that seemed to be almost mystical. Yes, mystical, mysterious, romantic, strange, beautiful, unusual, sensual. We used to talk about the possibility of have known each other forms, at a different time in history.

In one scenario concerning us knowing each other in different forms, he suggested that I might've been a flower and he had been a hummingbird, sipping nectar from inside of me. I can still remember the hot flash that shot through me when he suggested that.

One day he spent an hour talking to me about the royal lives we have shared in ancient Egypt, as members of the Egyptian royal family, being brother and sister and being married to each other. He could always make me feel as though we were on a different wave length from the rest of the world. That's why I say mystical. The contrast between my dead husband, the practical guy, and Leon, the romantic, was clear cut. Jim never advised me to do anything that wasn't practical, reasonable. Leon constantly encouraged me to do whatever my impulses led me to. He was definitely the most romantic man I'd ever met. It was an unusual romanticism, one that I could never prepare myself for.

He'd show up at the library with a bouquet of withered flowers and tell me that he had saved them for me all week. I'd laugh so hard that it would be impossible to take the gift seriously. Or to be angry with him. His sense of romanticism included laughter. I'd always wind up laughing with him. He'd make certain that I would crack up when we were together.

Leon had a strange and unusual idea of what was beautiful, sensual. A small example? He discovered the smell of skunks in Augusta. "I don't ever remember smellin' anything as exotic as this back home." Believe it or not, he found a place that sold skunk-based 'perfume' and bought me a beautifully designed, one-ounce vial of the stuff.

"It's an unusual smell, isn't it?" he asked.

I was forced to agree with him. It did have an unusual smell. But that was something of what made him the different kind of person he is.

It was the source of this incredible charm that no one was immune to. Leon's atmosphere was sensual, that was something that I began to understand from the very beginning, but I wasn't aware of it until he explained it to me.

"Simone, all is sensual, except for that which is not. And that's not something we want to buy into, is it?"

That's the way he talked about sensuality, as though it was supposed to be natural part of your life. I'd never experienced that concept before. He would look at me sometimes in the strangest way. I felt as though he was make love to me with his eyes. Leon was the most exciting man I'd ever met, but deep down, I knew we would never be together. We had too many obstacles to overcome; age, differences of outlook, class levels, what constitutes a good life, the Bohemian who can't take the middle class lady into his lifestyle. Too many obstacles. But we tried our best to do what we could.

Chapter 8

"What can I say? I got an honorable discharge, thank God, tripped back home and sat up dreaming about Muntuna for three whole months. I wrote her letters but I discovered that was waste of time. Her response to one of my ten page passion pleas was a post card, "Thanks for your letter, wish you were here again."

Tuna could say so much in so few words. My phone calls were more stimulating but filled with frustration.

"Tuna, how you doin', baby."

"I'm okay."

"Uhh, how's your Mom 'n Dad?"

"They okay."

"Do you miss me?"

"That's silly question, you know I do."

After three months of this kind of emotional shadow boxing, I knew I was not going to be satisfied until we were together. I called her one night and asked her if she would marry me. There was a lot of crackling and static on the line. they were having bad weather down there.

"Huh? I can't hear you too good?"

"I said, will you marry me?"

"Oh."

"Oh, what? Yes or no?"

"Uh huh."

She could be the most exasperating woman in the history of womankind, but she had my nose wide open. (And quiet as it's kept, she's still got my nose open.)

"Well, when do you want to do it?" Snap, crackle, pop, snackle.

"Do what?"

"Get married!"

"When do you want to do it?"

"How about next month?"

"Will I have to come up there, up Nawth?"

I had already made the decision to move down there. Atlanta ('the New York of duh Souf') was filled with opportunities and besides, I just couldn't see Muntuna in Philly. She needed heat, magnolia blossoms, soft voices, a more gentle approach to life around her. "No baby, I'm coming back down there. We can move to Atlanta. I've already applied for a job with a real estate agency."

I went back the following month to tie the knot. Strange sort of feeling to back to a place like that. when I was in the service, prowling around the town like a tom cat on weekend passes, I had a bit of a snobbish attitude toward the place. It was, first of all, the first medium sized town I'd ever spent any time in and it was Southern to the bone. It was like being in a place where the rhythm was so much different than the one I was used to, they all seemed to be moving in slow motion. And now I was smack dab in the middle of it.

We had the wedding in a First Holiness Baptist Church, Reverend A. T. Jackson presiding. Muntuna invited all of her girlfriends, who came loaded with enough cheap perfume on their bodies to make the little church smell like a third rate 'hoe house. But that was okay. It added a flavor to the whole thing. Simone, Mrs. Williams, the librarian came. I managed to have a few words with her at the reception.

"Mrs. Williams, how are you?"

"You may call me Simone. And I'm fine. Congratulations."

"Thank you."

"Tuna is a fine young woman. She's a bit backwards, as I'm sure you must know by now, like a lot of our younger people, but she has a good mind and she's honest."

"Like you."

She laughed her special little laugh.

"When have you heard from Leon?" I jammed on her.

"Oh, yesterday, as a matter of fact. 'Scuse me, there's Mr. Hollis. He's had one of our big picture books out a month overdue now."

I was really curious, but I couldn't have my curiosity satisfied. She had moved away from my questions. Very oblique move, very. Leon and I had exchanged letters for a few minutes. You know how it is. You've shared this gruesome experience and you exchange comments about it for a while and then other things creep in. I had asked him about his relationship with Simone, but he was always evasive. 'We're in touch.'

Meanwhile, there was Muntuna and my move to Atlanta. Real interesting place, Atlanta. Then and now. Here we have this beautiful, slow moving little town (Augusta) with trees drooping everywhere and there, ninety-two miles up the road, is this bustling, hustlin' city. I wouldn't call it a New York, a Big Apple. I'd call it the little apple.

I scored within the first year of my move, got in on four major real estate development deals and a half of a piece of another one. Muntuna was an even bigger score, I was delightfully surprised. Let me digress here for a bit.

I dug Tuna, let there be no doubt in anybody's mind, but what I thought I was digging her about turned out to be something else. Sure, she was fine. She had these *grand mal* hips 'n stuff, and that's what I felt I was on to. But then, precious lamb, I begin to discover other traits that I'd never really noticed before. The sister, for example, was tight. I mean, she could squeeze a nickel until the eagle screamed. I'd never seen anybody do what she could do with a dollar. Atlanta was the Big City for her and she was determined not to let anybody take advantage of her.

"Herb, I don't think we oughta go grocery shoppin' at that sto' again."

"Why, baby, it seems like a pretty good market to me."

"It looks good, but I notice that they're chargin' ten cents more per pound for puc'corns than the other sto's."

"How do you know?"

"'Cause I went around, that's how." Tight and shrewd. Slightly innocent, but shrewd. She showed me something about what it really meant to 'save yourself.'

"I know what you thought. You thought I was just one of those loose country girls who would just lay down for the first man who came along."

"No, I didn't really think that."

"You lyin' through yo' teeth, Herbert!"

"Well, let's say that you're right. What made you give in to me?"

"I was saving myself for the right man and I knew, when I met you, that you were the right man."

"As the saying goes, 'it's momma's baby and daddy's maybe.' I'm just joking, Tuna."

81

There's no way I could doubt what this beautiful sister laid on me. And is still laying on me after all these years. Oddly enough, despite the fact that we were only a two-hour bus ride from Augusta and Muntuna kept regular contact with her folks, we were in another world. Whenever she made a visit home, she'd check the latest gossip and bring it all back.

"I was talking to Lucille and she was tellin' me that the mailman, George Franklin, delivers a lot of letters to Miz Williams from Leon."

"So, they're still in touch, huh?"

"Seem to be."

We named our first child, a boy, Leon. I wrote Leon about it. "We just had a manchild down here, bro'...and, of course, we named him Leon." He sent a nice little gift, a hundred dollar bill, and faded back into the woodwork again. Leon did that a lot. We'd have a rapid fire exchange of letters for a while and then nothing.

I gained ten pounds and joined a few prestigious clubs and stuff. And, as everybody knows, we struggled through the sixties and won a few civil rights. I went down South for the love of a woman and to be really honest about it, I hated it at first. We're not talking about segregation 'n stuff like that. No matter where you grew up in this country, you've experienced prejudice, bigotry and segregation, if you're Black. No, it wasn't that. It was one thing to be stationed down there, in the Army, and it was another thing to live there. I was frustrated a lot at first, by slowness of things. In some ways I could've been a foreigner in some slow movin', third world country. Would you believe? I actually had to reschedule a whole bunch of meeting with a very important client because he had to go cat fishing.

Of course, early on, it had to do with not being a member of a good ol' boys club, too.

Muntuna gave me a lot of help in that area. "Herb, you can't be drivin' so hard on people the way you do. Take it easy, you gon' be wearin' yourself out."

By the time we had our fourth child, another boy, that we named Mongo, I had learned how to do business, Southern style. In some ways it was almost an imitation of what I'd heard about the Hollywood scene. I'd call a prospective client, we'd make an appointment to 'do lunch.' Or meet for a hot game of tennis. Or arrange to have a discreet talk in the library during one of those Peachtree dinner parties that someone was always having, is always having.

What the hell can I say? I made it. I have four beautiful children, a wife who keeps me chilled out and happy, a big fine home and all the perks that go with having fourteen major credit cards. Last year, when we made our third trip to the continent, I strolled along the beach in Ghana, thinking about how lucky I've been. I forget who said it, but there's an old saying, "if a man can say that he has two good menfriends and a faithful wife, he's been blessed." Well, I can definitely say I have a faithful wife and the last time I heard form one of my menfriends, brother Leon, he was tripping around Europe, spending the money he'd earned from his book.

That reminds me. I'm going to have to rag his ass a little bit. What kind of a friend is it that can trip off to every corner of the planet but can't make a simple trip to Atlanta?

Chapter 9

I don't know why, but I could never make Herb understand why I couldn't trip down to Georgia. Going down there would've meant Simone and, well, it's a whole 'nother story. I felt like someone who had pulled off major league *coup* by escaping from the Army without going to the stockade. Lord knows I came pretty damn close.

Herb got out of the Army and out of Georgia and returned to Georgia, all praise be to the charms of Muntuna. I got out and got high, and stayed high for a month. There was so much I was trying to forget. The very thought of where I had just spent the past two years used to cause me to break into heavy sweat. I had come this close to being sent to Vietnam. It was '64, remember? I had to smoke and drink out a lot of negative shit. And after I did all that, I kept coming back to this love I had discovered down there. I couldn't get Simone out of my mind and I didn't know what to do about it.

I sobered up after a month and started thinking real hard on the sister. We began to exchange letters. It was really a tricky, ticklish ass situation. We couldn't figure out what to do with each other. I knew that I wanted to be with her, but, to be honest, I didn't really have a handle on how I wanted to be with her. I almost envied Herb and his situation with Muntuna. He had fallen in love with his Georgia peach and tripped on down to be with her. He had married her.

It wasn't that definite between me and Simone. I was in love with her, that was certain, but I wasn't certain that I wanted to be married to her. I wasn't certain if she wanted to be married to me. The age thing didn't trouble me as much as the life style thing. I didn't see myself living in a small town and I couldn't imagine her trippin' around with me. I tripped out. It wouldn't take a world class shrink to figure out why I wanted to get out of America for a while. I had served two years in the Army, the whole time in racist Georgia (except for basic at Fort Ord) and I felt the need for a different scene. Lots of shit was happenin' but I felt like someone on the sidelines, a spectator. I didn't feel compelled to be a good 'Negro' and go to school for a degree. Or wear a three piece suit and act nice. I wanted something else.

Simone was wonderful to me. Supportive, loving. Whenever we spoke on the phone she always encouraged me to do whatever I felt I wanted to do.

"Simone, I've saved a little money. I'm going to a little town on the west coast of Mexico for a while. I'm going to be a writer. I'm going down there to write a book."

"That sounds like a wonderful idea, Leon."

It was really crazy. I remember being in this little village on the west coast of Mexico, writing this novel by oil lamp, thinking about this beautiful woman. It was so bad, I fantasized about her. I fantasized about us living together

85

but I could never place us in any particular place. I could never really figure out what we'd do together and, I guess—that was the crux of our problem.

I took myself through a lot of changes about Simone. We would have long periods when we wouldn't communicate at all, no cards, no letters, no phone calls and then, as though nothing had happened, we would slip right back into the groove. I returned from Mexico during one of these 'open periods' and got married. Don't ask me why. It just seemed like it was the right thing to do at the moment. The sister I married was beautiful, inside and out. She had to be to deal with my madness. I went through about five jobs during the two years we were married and wrote another novel and a collection of short stories.

Simone replied to my letters and when I told her I had gotten married she wished me well. When I was divorced she allowed me to cry on her shoulder, long distance. I had never known a woman like Simone and I'm sure I will never know a woman like her again. During moments of extreme soberness and lucidity, I would sit and try to think of all the reasons why I should go back to Georgia and propose to Simone. And then I'd sit and think of just as many reasons why I shouldn't go. It was during one of these periods of ambivalence that I sold one of my novels.

I went berserk for a while. Suddenly, I was published writer. I didn't know what to do. I decided to move to California. It seemed like the right thing to do for a published writer. Strangely, Simone never faded from my mind. I could spend a month rippin' 'n runnin' all over California and then, as though a giant tuning fork had vibed on me, I would have to write or phone Simone. There were times when I could sense her distress with me. It was really something I sense not something she said. It was as though she were telling me, 'Look, Leon, don't you know I'm the best thing that's

ever going to happen to you? Why don't you stop pootin'
around and come on back to me?'

Indecision drove me nuts. I felt committed to the idea of
being in love with her but I couldn't organize my brain to
receiving the actual thought of us being physically together.
Meanwhile, she started doing a little trippin' of her own.
I was stunned when I received a card from Alaska. "Dear
Leon, as you can see, I'm in Alaska, hope things are going
well with you, Simone." I walked around in a semi-jealous
state for a few days, imagining that she was up in Juneau
with somebody. A week later, she explained in a letter that
one of her daughters had gotten married and moved to
Alaska. she had gone for a visit. I was relieved, but slightly
shook. I don't know why, but for some weird reason, I
always assumed that she would be there for me. God, what
a fool I was.

"Lotus Land" gave me a few unexpected perks. I was in
the Watts Writers Workshop (the catalyst was the Watt
Rebellion of '65) and got into a groovy one-shot movie deal.
For the first time in my entire life, I had more than a thousand
bucks in my bank account. I should've been happy. I wasn't.
I spent days wandering around Griffith Park, trying to figure
out what to do with myself.

I wrote my ass off, heart grinding scenarios of unrequited
love, mystery stories, adventure tales, crazy science fiction.
I was on a roll. It was a baffling time for me. I was having
what amounted to a moderate amount success but I wasn't
happy. It seemed, in some strange way, that I was in a deep,
soulful depression and nothing could bring me out of it. After
three to four years of this kind of stuff, I knew it was too
late, that we'd never be together. I brooded a lot and went
off to Spain for a year. Maybe my soul knew what I needed.
It was either going to be Flamenco or the Blues. I think I
subconsciously chose Flamenco to brood under because the

words were in a foreign language. I knew what the music was about, but I didn't understand all the words. It was just right. We continued writing each other.

There were times when she seemed to be able to read my mind, to jump in behind me and stroke me out from thousands of miles away. "Dear Leon, I have the feeling that you are worrying yourself to distraction over here, if you really feel the need to worry."

It, this soul play we had going on, influenced my work to such an extent that one reviewer called me "the Miles Davis of African-American novelists."

Finally, one day, I just decided to stop telephoning and writing. I made a conscious decision and I suffered for days because of it. I based my decision on two things. Number one, I wanted to 'free' her. I knew, as long as I continued to hold out the possibility of us being together she would never get into anything serious with anyone else. I felt I owed her that opportunity. Number two, I wanted to 'free' myself. There were no other women in my life, on the serious level, and I knew that there would never be, as long as we maintained this thread.

She seemed to agree with me by the simple act of not questioning why I didn't reply to her last letter. It was almost as simple as that. One day, we were exchanging lovely little postcards and red hot letters, and the next day, we weren't. It went like that, literally.

I can't say that my decision was the right one, or that it gave me peace of mind. No, none of that happened. As a matter of fact, since I spoke with her, or wrote to her, there are days when her vibe is on me so heavily, I feel that I'm hallucinating.

In some ways, Simone reminds me of the saying they have about the existence of God. "If *She* didn't exist, we would've been compelled to invent her."

Chapter 10

The very first thing I have to say is that I love Leon, and I always will. I can say that with ease, because he never gave me any cause not to love him. When he first realized I was emotionally vulnerable, he could have taken advantage of me but he didn't and I'll always love him for that. I mean, let's face it, how many men will step away from hurting a woman, if they have a physical desire for her?

I watched him go through lots of changes when he was stationed down here, changes that would've turned some people into a horror show. The thing he had going on with that awful sergeant, for example, the one who forced him to become a fireman. Can you imagine how he must've felt, being forced to be on duty for twenty-four hours at a time? I cried for him any number of times. But I never heard him complain, he just took whatever and kept on moving.

Despite the fact that I was older than Leon, I always had the feeling that he was older. "It comes from my 'street-pertise.''' he used to say.

He was so wise in so many ways. He taught me how to kiss. Isn't that a ridiculous admission for a woman my age to make? My first husband, Lord rest his unromantic soul, never took a lot of time to do things like kiss. His idea of a romantic evening was to jump on top of me and have an orgasm. I never confessed to Leon, after he started his kissing lessons, that I think I was coming as close to having an orgasm as I'd ever had in my life.

He was so full of fun and stories. I'll never forget the one he used to tell about his woman who lived in India who hadn't eaten any food in twenty years.

"But, Leon," I asked him, "how does she live?"

"She draws her energy directly from the sun, Simone, directly from the sun."

"But what happens when the sun isn't shining?"

"She fasts on days like that."

Now whether or not this was a true story, I never found out. But it didn't matter whether or not the story was true. The important thing to me is that he would think to tell me a story like that.

And the jokes. I knew I was going to hear at least a dozen crazy jokes whenever he was around. Example?

"Knock, knock!"

"Who's there?"

"Orange."

"Orange who?"

"Orange you glad to see me?"

Silly, huh? But nice. I think people, especially serious thinking adults need to lighten their burdens with a little silliness every now and then. Leon understood that quite well. He understood things about me that I barely understood about myself. I couldn't really understand what he saw in me, to be frank, at first. I hadn't been anywhere, I hadn't done

90

anything. I couldn't kiss.

"Simone, you're special, you know what I mean? You're special." Let someone tell you something like that often enough and you'll begin to believe. Take my work for it. He was the first man who had made the effort to make me feel special and I appreciated that, I really did.

We could talk about so many things, God! How refreshing it was to be able to talk to someone about a book or a latest Hollywood scandal or whatever. I was always amazed at how much he knew about so many different things.

"That's 'street-pertise,' Simone. If you grow up on the South and West sides of Chicago, there's a lot of shit you learn early in the game, real early,if you want to survive."

To be perfectly honest, I'd never given a lot of thought to number of things, 'til he brought them to my attention. Stuff about geopolitics, Eurocentric educational patterns, Egyptology, Asian art, Tibetan mystery stories, sound vibrational healing, Capoeira, Afro-Cuban drumming. I could go on and on about the esoterica that he knew about.

He was a soldier, 'a reluctant draftee,' he called himself, and was completely disrespectful of what he called 'designer authority.' "Why should I grant them respect for making my life miserable?"

Of course, that's one of the reasons he wound up working as a fireman in his unit, but he made me understand the necessity for rebellion. "Somebody has got to rebel, Simone. People stick their faces into the boob tube and just hang in there, sucking up crap 'til they're blue in the face."

We'd have disagreements, arguments I should say, arguments. But they were always constructive. He wasn't the type to simply disagree for the sake of being disagreeable. sometimes, he was right. Sometimes, I was right. The disagreements were usually philosophical, not hard core.

"Simone, don't you understand what an effect it would

91

have on these ol' white thangs down here if we knocked a few of them off every month?''

"Yes, I do clearly understand. We'd be up to our hips in black bodies within a week.''

I think the biggest problem we had was what he was going to do about his life. I was concerned about him. I used to tell him, "Leon, you can't just go around for the rest of your life rebelling. You've got to commit yourself to something that's going to be beneficial to yourself and mankind.''

He expressed a deep interest in writing, but at that time, he had only written a few short stories. "Leon, a real writer writes everyday, not just when he's inspired to write. It's a craft, not a bake-off.'' He understood and agreed with me. In many ways, he was the most mysterious, romantic, strange, unusual man I'd ever met.

We discussed the possibility of having known each other in different forms, at a different time in history. One of his favorite scenarios was that I had been a beautiful flower and he was a hummingbird, sipping nectar from inside of me. I still recall the hot flash that shot through me when he suggested that.

Another time, he spent an hour talking about the royal lives we had shared in those days. On other occasions, he'd show up at the library with a bouquet of withered flowers and make some kind of super gallant speech. I'd be forced to laugh at all this and that would make his day. He could be utterly serious but at the same time his sense of romanticism definitely included laughter. I've never met anyone who could laugh so hard at other people. And at himself.

Leon's atmosphere was sensual, that was something I began to understand from the very beginning, but I couldn't clearly put a finger on it until he explained it to me. "Simone, everything is sensual, of the senses, except for that which it not. And that's not something we want to buy into, is it not?''

He'd look at me sometime, as though he was making love to me with his eyes. Those were the times when I really and truly understood the deeper meaning of the word "love."

Finally, one day, inevitably, he got his honorable discharge from the service and returned to Chicago. We had gotten together for a long lunch at Wong's Restaurant the day before his discharge, to talk about what was going to happen between us. As usual, Wong's food was greasy and not very appetizing. Unusually, Leon's talk was not very satisfying either. It was a strained two hours we spent together. I really can't recall anything of any significance that we talked about and the next day he was gone.

We exchanged letters and he called almost every day for months after he left. There were gaps when neither one of us communicated by letter or phone but we always stayed in touch. His friend, Herb, married one of our hometown girls and moved down here, to Atlanta. I went to their wedding, but I avoided talking to Herb about Leon, quite diplomatically, I thought. Herb wanted him to come down for a visit but Leon resisted. I could understand that. It was as though there were scents in the air that no one could identify.

I knew Leon loved me and I loved him but we couldn't put a title on it, in a manner of speaking. I had children already, a lifestyle that I was comfortable with, but aside from all that, there was something to do with a kind of insecurity on both sides. I don't know. When he called to tell me that he was going to Mexico for a while, to write, I was torn between being happy and depressed. One side of me wanted to rejoice and the other side wanted to ask, "Why not come to Georgia to write?"

But I didn't want him to feel that he should be obligated to me in any way. We both found ourselves going through changes all the time. I could sense it.

He wrote me long, beautiful letters from Mexico. I kept them. I still have them. Needless to say, I was shocked when we wrote to tell me that he was getting married a few months after he returned from Mexico. Why lie? I was terribly hurt, but in some crazy way a rational part of me felt that way. We had never become platonic friends, nor had we ever discussed the possibility. And we never did. I felt just as neutral about his divorce when he wrote me about it. And I was relieved. Strangely, I'd never even thought about remarrying, not even out of spite.

In a way, I felt married to Leon. Isn't that weird? When he sent me an autographed copy of his book, I felt tempted to go down to Wong's Restaurant and have one of those martinis that Leon liked so much. I shared his triumphs and his failures as though we were together and yet we weren't.

He opened a few psychic doors for me, in a manner of speaking. Before he came along, I would never have considered taking a trip anywhere. When Shirley, my youngest, got married, I hopped on a plane to Juneau, Alaska, like it was a bus trip to Atlanta. I give Leon credit for that.

He was achieving a moderate success as a writer during this period and constantly expressing his frustration with life. I sensed that the frustration had to do with his ambivalence concerning our relationship and I tried, as often as I could, to let him off the hook. After two years of this kind of thing, I had a strong suspicion that we were never going to get together. When he wrote to tell me that he was going to live in Spain for a while, my suspicions were confirmed.

One day I suddenly realized that we hadn't exchanged a letter in over three months and I hadn't heard his voice in over six months. A cold feeling came over me. I felt that I knew exactly what he was doing. He was freeing me from the idea of us being together. He was releasing himself from the possible title of hypocrite.

In some ways, despite the fact that it's been five years since we've communicated, I feel closer to Leon than ever before. Like he used to say, "If our relationship had never existed, we would've had to take some kind of wonder drug, to hallucinate it into being."

The only thing I could add to that is that I feel better about my life for having had one Leon in it, than no Leon at all.

ONE LOVE

BY LEON CARSON

DEDICATION

There are times, moments in the history of our brief lives that cannot be recorded normally, they require the creation of a work of art.

I wrote this for Simone...

Theolonius Seminole Kuumba Brown, better known by the cognoscenti as Kuumba because he played the piano better than anyone else in the Western Hemisphere, liked to announce, dead pan, that he and his partner, Tony Nia Jones, had arrived well before the *Mayflower*.

"We came before Columbus, whoever he was, found a relatively inexpensive place on the Southside of Chicago and settled in for the winter."

Tony, friend from the beginning, was prone to cast a slight smile at the slightly bewildered expressions that blanketed Kuumba's audiences. Theolonius usually started his performances off with abstract bits of humor that were laced with facts. Many of his long time fans looked forward to his dissertations. Theolonius was bringing them a lifetime of memories in one night.

"I'm only playing here one night, tonight, so if you didn't catch me tonight, you may never see me 'cause I'll be gone."

Tony found himself writing for his money but decided not to call himself a writer.

"Titles are so limiting."

Kuumba practiced the piano by the hour, but didn't consider himself a superior pianist, despite the acclaim from all sections of the musical world and his own self mocking statements. "Art Tatum was a piano player. How can I call myself a piano player, if I don't play as well as he played?" He confused some people with his logic.

They took pride in being self-directed, "careerless," in the sense of not trying to claw other folks' eyes out in order to say that they had "made it," creative, mad, free. They weren't Ron Karenga followers but they had decided to take his seven principles; umoja-unity, kugichagulia-self determination, ujima-collective work/responsibility, ujamaa-cooperative economics, nia-purpose, kuumba-creativity, iman-faith, seriously.

"It may not be the perfect set of rules to go by, but it beats the Golden Rule. Whoever has the gold, rules."

"Dig that."

Tony Nia Jones, 'Brother Nia' to his close friends, was the one with the "purpose" and Kuumba supplied the creativity. They were a team (Tony as promoter and agent for both of them), loved doing what they did and took it seriously even when they didn't seem to be doing it. They were seduced by wanderlust at an early age.

"Kuumba, you know something, man? We oughta pull outta here, fly off into the stratosphere, become world citizens for a while."

They had discovered the power of purpose and creativity at seventeen, interwoven their wills and wound up in Mexico City. It was their stepping place. Tony had caught on with a small, independent, avant garde publishing company that was willing to publish as many of his books as he would/could channel their way. He put together a series of sequels entitled "The Jive Time Chronicles," the story of two brothers who had decided to be different. Theolonius Seminole Kuumba Brown only needed a slightly tuned piano to make his mark.

"Tony, you know what, man? We are just pure idee magic, you know what I mean?"

"I do know, my brother. I do know."

They seemed to be capable of attracting cash flows because they had decided not to bog themselves down with the horrible business of being poor.

One evening, under the pressures of paying for a week in a super swank hotel, they had simply decided to become invisible. It didn't matter that they had to leave a closet full of shoes and suits.

"Where to now, brother man?"

"Why don't we keep on going South for a bit?

They paused on the tenth floor of the Hotel Colón in Panama City for a year, time enough for Tony to finish a novel and for Kuumba to become a pianistic drawing card.

"Nia, we better move on, we're beginning to get fat and complacent here. I think the challenge is beginning to slip away from us."

They shipped out of the Canal Zone the following week on a luxury freighter, winding up in the city of Alicante, Spain. A farsighted producer purchased the rights to two of *The Jive Time Chronicles*, giving them trash bags full of money.

"How many *pesetas* does this equal?"

"Check it out, fifty thousand times one hundred and eighty five *pesetas*."

"Woww! That's a lot of coins in anybody's language."

"Yeahh, it is. We better start giving some of it away as soon as possible."

They received the first real romantic threat to their

comradeship on a trip to Madrid.

"Tony, Tony, I'm in love, man. You hear me?! I'm in love!"

"I know, with the piano."

"No, this is with a woman, a real honest to goodness woman!"

"Sounds serious, run it down to me.

"Okay, check this out. I go up to the Penthouse Bon, over there on Avenida San Juan, the ritzy joint. I felt like weaving a spell on some people. You know how that creativity will come down on you when you least expect it."

"I know, I know all about it."

"Anyway, the manager sees me coming, knows that I'm about to play them all the way into the next feeling, and waves me away from the piano.

"What?!"

"Yeahh, he says...sorry, Senor Kuumba, the Empire Room has been taken over by the Prince. 'The Prince? What prince?' I ask him. 'Prince Fuad Al-Hassan.' At this point, a trio that looked like they just stepped straight out of the *Arabian Nights* pause near by and ask the manager—'what's happening?' The manager explains who I am. I must say he really laid it on, and that I've come to play their piano but, of course, he tells them, he cannot allow me to play the piano this evening because The Prince has reserved the room. The smallest one of the trio pulls his silk scarf away from his face and says, 'Of course the American is allowed to play. I would like to hear him.'"

"This little dude is The Prince himself, the other two are his bodyguards. 'What kind of music do you play?' he asks me. 'Basically, extraterrestrial African-American Classical,' I tell him, 'influenced by Monk and Tatum.' His eyes light up behind his shades. 'Ahhhhh, Ta-tum, Art Ta-Tum, my father had many of his records.' So, that's how I wound up playing for the Prince of Shakebaby, or whatever the place is called."

"I'm puzzled. Where does the love thang come in?"

"I'm gettin' to it, I'm gettin' to it. During the course of creating one of these little spells I've been known to create sometimes, when I'm really on my form, a couple of princes' bodyguards leads four women into the room and seats them directly behind me. Would you believe?! They were swaddled up from head to toe in material. I'm pretty certain it was silk. Unreal, huh? In this day'n age?"

"Yeah, they still have stuff like that in some places."

"Tell me about it. I'm playin' my ass off, switching from "Night of the Goldfish" to "Soweto Stomp" with little touches of Ravel and Debussy thrown in, you know, just doodlin', smelling this gorgeous perfume. And that's when I looked up in the mirror over the piano, right smack dab into the blackest, most lustrous, sexiest eyes I have ever seen in my life. I had to pause in the middle of a heavy run, to pull myself together and right there, this lovely melody swam up into my consciousness . . . I'm calling it 'Dark Eyes in the Mirror.'"

Tony smiled. Kuumba's titles didn't always offer a true reflection of what his music was about.

"Then what happened?"

"Well, nothing overt. I just exchanged eye songs with her, to let her know that I was opening my soul to receive her vibes. It was pretty close to adultery, to tell you the truth. The next thing I know, the prince has gotten pissed, I wasn't aware that he had checked our mirror action out, laid a thousand dollars on me and I'm being gently escorted out of the Empire Room, midway through my second rendition of 'Dark Eyes in the Mirror.'"

They laughed about his 'love affair' all the way to Rio de Janiero.

103

"Kuumba, my friend, I think we need a change of scenery, back to something tropical." Rio de Janiero was where Tony met his 'Dark Eyes in the Mirror.' Her name was Zena and she wasn't polymarried to a jealous Middle Eastern.

Rio de Janiero throbbed.

"Mannnn, this is where we should've tripped to when we first left the States. This scene is live! You hear me, brother man. Live!"

They secured a suite in a semi-fancy hotel and worked out a gig for "Kuumba" in a jazz club six blocks away. Tony was writing the first of eight articles on the state of the African-Brazilian culture for a scholarly Black magazine published in New Orleans, and ghosting a novel for a wealthy African-American businessman who wanted to experience what creativity was about. The pulse of the city intrigued them. They had days and nights when it seemed as though they had wandered into an incredible party, stocked with all kinds of people, music, a kind of fever that gave the impression that everyone was dancing and enjoying themselves, even the people sleeping under newspapers in doorways.

And the beautiful women!

"Tony, did you check that one out?!"

"I most certainly did."

They strolled the streets staring at women who seemed to be composites of every recognizable racial group, pausing for delicacies in small sidewalk cafes, excited by the rhythms that ebbed and flowed with the briskly shuffling crowds.

Kuumba had pulled twenty different rhythms in on top of his own stuff and Tony had written a collection of songs that reflected their total sense of place at being where they were, physically and mentally.

"Damn! Tony, don't you wish more of the brothers 'n sisters would break out of their concrete slave coffins and come here. Or go somewhere, other than New York?''

"I wished things like that, a few years ago but I gave it up. You can't do anything for people that they don't want to do for themselves.''

Milton Janela, the owner of the Oba Oba Club, a wise businessman, upped Kuumba's salary with a larger slice of the weekend house pie.

"It is only right, Theoloniuse, because you are such a superb musician.''

"I can certainly dig where you're comin' from, Milton. And obrigado.''

They had been in Rio a month before they started thinking about other areas of the country.

"People talk about Bahia a lot, what do you think?''

"I think it would be real hip to trip that way after we get back from Africa.''

"Africa, huh? When're we leaving?''

"How 'bout next month?

"Sounds like a winner to me.''

They could do that with each other, a facet of the understanding they shared. It was like a code, it kept life sparkling and kept them on the move, following their self-designed, nomadic lifestyle.

It all happened before Zena. And it happened at the Oba Oba Club.

Kuumba, under the influence of a half thimble of Cachaca and the memory of Copacabana Beach at high noon, was taking the club patrons through a series of musical tunnels, carefully layered textures of samba and Mississippi soul. Tony saw her enter, sitting at his usual table, the one he shared with Kuumba between sets, whenever he was on the scene. He watched Milton, the owner, stroll over to her and escort her to a choice table, an unusual concession for him to make.

105

"If a single woman comes into Oba Oba, she must be prepared to be treated like a single woman."

Tony studied her carefully, analyzing and admiring. A walnut shaded vision in snow white. The image fixed itself in his mind. A gorgeous African woman, not thin, full hipped, large lipped, almond eyed, full of slow rhythms and quick movements. She seemed to be oblivious to the flirtatiously warm looks of the Brazilians and the music that Kuumba suddenly made up to honor her presence. Tony exchanged a coded look with Kuumba that expressed his telepathic appreciation. Kuumba twinkled a few notes to him, to let him know that he was already enchanted. She was obviously an African-American, he could tell that. There was something about the brother and sisters. He and Kuumba had discussed the subject often. There was a certain kind of hipness, rather than being simply aloof. It was harder to tell if a person was European, if he kept his sunglasses on.

"I don't know, blood, there's just something about us, you know? The way we carry ourselves."

Kuumba ended his first set with a unique rendition of "January in Rio," one of the twenty new pieces he and Tony had put together since their arrival. At the end of the set the audience gave him a standing ovation, something he hated.

"I don't think any living human being should be given a standing ovation, that should be reserved for great people who've died."

Tony focused on her body language. She was beautifully built, not just simply a woman with a fantastic shape. And there was a simple, direct, natural way about her. Kuumba strolled away from the stage, nodding pleasantly to his fans, exchanging a handshake here and there.

"Man, what do you make of that goddess-woman over there?" he whispered. Tony ignored the question, trying to put together a reason for meeting her. He hit on it.

"Kuumba, this gorgeous sister is obviously a fan of yours and I think she deserves to be introduced to you." Kuumba was in complete agreement.

"How do you want to do it? Should we go to her table, send a note to her table, or what?" They huddled over their glasses of batida, trying to come up with the right approach. They arrived at an honest solution.

"Hey, let's just go over and introduce ourselves. We do want to meet this person, don't we?" They came up out of their huddle to discover she was gone. They stared into each others faces, almost in panic. She was gone.

Kuumba called/signalled to Milton, the owner, calling him over.

"Milt, where did she go, man?" The owner, a man with a sense of humor, looked around innocently.

"She? Who?"

They moved toward him, mock ferocity on their faces, hands curled into strangling claws. "Ohh oh," he recoiled in humorous, mock fear, "the beautiful *preta*."

"Yeahhh, the sister."

"Ahhh yes, that one. She is very beautiful, is she not?"

"Yes, she is. Now, when did she leave? Where did she go?"

Milton folded his arms across his chest, enjoying their North American anxiety. "I think she may have left, you know, perhaps to experience other things in our beautiful city." He smiled slyly at the distressed looks that spread across their faces. "Or perhaps she simply made a trip to make a pee pee. You know?"

She cooled out their anxiety as she glided back to her table. They sighed with relief. They hadn't lost her. Several Brazilian men, with and without their wives, stared with envy as Tony "Nia" Jones and Theolonius Seminole Kuumba Brown made their way to the beautiful woman's table.

"Please excuse us for intruding on your privacy, but we

107

felt compelled to come over and welcome you to Rio."

"That's very gracious of you. And, of course, its a privilege to meet the very talented Mr. Brown."

Kuumba unleashed a rare ear-to-ear smile. "Thank you for the compliment. If you're not expecting anyone else, we'd like to join you."

"I'd be honored."

Milton, following the nuances, rushed chairs over at Kuumba's casual signal and surprised them with a bottle of his best cachaca.

"Please accept this, with my warmest compliments." Tony and Kuumba exchanged startled looks. Milton Janela, giving something away?

"Thank you, thank you very much."

Milton poured a drink for each of them into the thumb sized glasses that he used for his best cachaca. He also led the trio in a toast.

"To the future."

"To the future," they echoed. They swallowed a sip and savored the odd fire of the cane liquor.

"It's strong stuff, isn't it?" she announced, and dazzled both of them with a smile. The intermission was over.

"Well, gang, gotta get back on the job. It was a pleasure meeting you...uhh...miss?"

"My name is Zena."

"Zena?"

"Just Zena."

Tony stared at her profile as she watched Kuumba return to the piano. From time to time he paused, turned to the audience and chatted for a moment. One admirer called him a Black Victor Borge, noting that his comments were not always funny.

"How did you two know I wasn't Brazilian?"

"I don't know how to explain it. It's the kind of thing you

feel. Like you knowing that we were brothers from the States. Kuumba joined the conversation with a piano reading of the *Saeta* that Miles Davis had made popular on his album, "Sketches of Spain." He played all of the parts and when he paused under the balcony where the Gypsy was singing her "arrow of song" into the heart of the Virgin, some of the more serious Catholics in the club looked as though they were about to cry.

"He is really phenomenal, isn't he?"

Tony nodded in agreement, feeling a twinge of jealousy. She was warm, gorgeous, down to Earth, full of good vibes. She made him feel that life was better in her presence. The night ended with the three of them sharing bowls of shrimp soup in an all night restaurant. They felt the need to know where she was from, who she really was, what she was doing in Brazil, where she was headed? She seemed content to simply accept them as she found them. Cleverly, she circumnavigated their questions without seeming to be evasive.

"Awww c'mon, guys, who wants to burden himself with all that stuff?"

After a couple of fun filled days and three late, late nights, they had become a warm trio, a trio that Tony tried to convert into a duo whenever he got the chance.

"Uhhh, Kuumba, my brother, I thought you had to practice."

"Nahhhh, not this afternoon. I'll get back to it this evening."

After a week, matters came to a head. They settled into it over nightcaps in their hotel room.

"Uhh, Kuumba? Don't get me wrong, brother, it ain't nothing personal, but about tomorrow?"

"What about tomorrow? We're doing a little picnic on Copacabana, right?"

They stared into each others eyes, two hip dudes from the 'hood, past games and fronts, they didn't try to chump each other off at any time.

"Well, that's what I wanted to talk to you about..."

"You want to be alone with Zena, huh?"

"If it's cool with you."

Kuumba released his special little smile. "Sounds like you got a hot spot for the sister, blood."

"Hot spot? Hot spot don't even come close to describing how I feel. My nose is wide open. And quiet as it's kept, your's is too."

Kuumba took a sip of his drink and solemnly nodded, no, no. "She doesn't have my nose open, not the way you mean. But I have to admit, I *was* feeling the way you feel, for a couple of days."

"Run that past me real slow, I'm missing something."

Kuumba avoided looking into Tony's eyes. "Well, how can I put this to you?"

"Anyway you want to. We've been through enough stuff together to be real with each other." Kuumba hesitated a few beats.

"It's just something I feel about the lady, Tony, just a feeling she's really superfine 'n all that, but I sense there's a missing part somewhere."

"And it's this missing part that turns you off?"

Kuumba looked frustrated. "I'm not exactly saying that she turns me off. It's something else. I can't really explain it. I mean, well, look at the way things are. She knows what our trip is but we don't know anything about her."

Tony was quiet, introspective, for a long moment. "All I know is that I love her, Kuumba, and I'm gonna ask her to join our trip."

"To be free, go to Africa? You think she's ready to do that, to trip?"

110

"I'll soon find out. You coming to the beach with us?"

"Not today, bro', I got a little sleeping to do."

"Later on, brotherman."

The day after their beach date melted into two weeks, Kuumba joined them from time to time, cracking off with jokes, being Theolonius Seminole Kuumba Brown. Tony was dealing with a sense of romance that he'd never known before. They started their mornings jogging on the beach and, midway into the third week, while he was taking a shower in her hotel room, they became lovers.

"Kuumba, I gotta rap with you, man. I've just had the most incredible thing happen."

"You and Zena made love today."

"How do you know? Did she tell you?"

"Be serious, brother, with the kind of expression you have on your face, nobody has to tell anybody anything."

"That obvious, huh?"

"I'd say so."

They stared at each other for a few moments, trying to pull pieces into place. Kuumba broke the spell.

"Have you broken the African trip on her head?"

"Not yet, but I will."

"Tony, you think this might get to be a little complicated? I mean, what if the lady doesn't relate to this sense of friendship. You're really like my brother, you know?"

"I know my lady well enough to know where her head is. When did we schedule ourselves to leave?"

"First of next month."

"That's only three weeks away."

"First of next month. You still game?"

"I wouldn't miss going to the Motherland for all the tea in China."

"But what about Zena?"

"Kuumba, you may know a lot about the piano, but not

111

about emotions. This is love, partner, love. This sister loves me and I'd bet anybody even money that she'll go anywhere with me."

Kuumba smiled slyly, skeptically. "I hope so, man. I hope so, for your sake."

Tony waited a full day, impatiently, before feeling Zena out about tripping off to Africa.

"It sounds like a beautiful idea, Tony, it really does. But what will you do, once you get there?"

"Glad you asked that. Kuumba and I have been planning to go to Ganibon and open up one of the hippest jazz clubs on the continent. We'll call it...we'll call it 'Zena's.'" He thought he detected a pained expression on her face, but brushed it aside.

"Tony, that's a big step, going to Africa."

"If you have any doubts about how honorable my intentions are, why don't we get married first?" He couldn't brush aside the look that bordered on sheer panic.

"Tony, I love you so much." From that point on their lovemaking seemed to intensify. Kuumba took note.

"From the look of those circles under your eyes, brotherman, you appear to be on your way to becoming a mere shell of a man."

"I'm sure it ain't the piano that's giving you that hollow look about the gills, either."

Rio de Janiero formed the cradle that they snuggled into. Zena wasn't convinced that they should get married. "Tony, it isn't that I don't want to be your wife, or anything like that."

"Well, what is it, baby? Kuumba is beginning to give funny looks, you know what I mean?" They laughed about the situation, but there as an edge to the laughter. During those moments their loving took on a frenzied air, as though they wanted to cocoon each other. Or swallow each other,

112

like sharks. He loved her unconditionally, knew she was his first real love and that he would never know another woman like her.

They were three days away from the kick off. "Zena," he pressed her one last time, "I want you to be my wife."

"Why don't we get married in Africa?" she suggested hesitantly. They celebrated her suggestion after Kuumba's last set.

"Okay, 'Father' Brown, I'm here to report good news. Zena has decided to make an honorable man out of me in Africa!"

"Heyyy! That's great! I was beginning to wonder if I was gonna have to bring the weight of public opinion down on this beautiful sister."

Milton Janela, the owner of Oba Oba, mourned Kuumba's going away with four bottles of champagne. And finally, it was the night before their day of departure. It was a warm, tropically humid night. They sprawled on the balcony sofa of Zena's seventh floor suite, each sparking light a pearl of visual pleasure to them, the sound of the city floating up to their ears. Some of the sounds were terrible, some beautiful, strange, weird, hard, lush, exotic, crazed, Brazilian.

"I thought I had seen some poverty stricken shit in my day, but this takes the cake."

"Yes, it is bad, isn't it? In the middle of all this beauty it's doubly hard to see people sleeping in the streets." Played out, they exchanged random thoughts.

"It's too bad the Portuguese fantasy has such a grip on this country. Can you imagine how cold blooded it would be to have a real Brazil, the African-Brazil stand up and be counted."

"It really is too bad. But our people down here, a lot of them, have been seduced and its going to take a while for them to get where we were twenty years ago. That is, unless

113

a bigger Abdias do Nascimento drops down on them. Yeahhh, the Portuguese put a very clever game together in Brazil.'' They stole words from each other with kisses that made oblique attacks, gazed out onto the glistening ocean, mystified by the majesty of Yemanja. They loved. And made extravagantly unplotted plans. They exchanged one last kiss at the door as she tried to pull a promise from him.

"Tony, no matter what happens, please promise that you'll always love me.''

"That doesn't sound like a difficult assignment.''

They were scheduled to meet at the airport at high noon for the 3:00 pm flight to Ganibon via Pan Am. Tony was feeling on the left side of manic by 1:15. Kuumba thumbed through a Brazilian version of life, strangely detached.

"Kuumba, she's not here, man! Maybe something happened.''

"Why don't you call her hotel and find out what's happening?''

The Brazilian telephone system, skipping and bouncing full of Samba rhythms, finally put him through to her hotel after ten minutes.

"Bom dia, Hotel Rio.''

"Miss Zena, por favor, Siete-uno-dos.''

"One moment, please.'' The clerk returned to the phone after five anxiety-ridden minutes. "The beautiful lady is checked out this day at eleven o'clock precisely.''

"Checked out! Where did she go?! Did she leave a forwarding address?! What do you mean she checked out?!''

"She checked out, sir.'' Click!

He hung up the phone and remained in place, staring into nothing. "Tony, Tony! Wake up, man! They're gaging you at the message center.'' They both raced to the message center. Tony's hand shook as he reached for the message.

"I'm Tony Nia Jones.'' The message was from Zena and

it was brief. "Dearest Tony, please forgive me for not being there with you. I couldn't make it. There is so much I should've explained but I didn't and now is not the time. Please forgive me for disappointing you. I'll always remember the way we were together."

"Tony, what's wrong, man? You okay?"

"Here, read this."

They were practically speechless during the long plane ride. Kuumba made a few efforts to talk over their plans to open the jazz club in Ganibon and gave up after he was ignored. They were approaching the coast of West Africa before he opened up with an anguished, "Why? Man, why?"

Kuumba could only shake his head, as completely puzzled by the woman's actions as Tony was.

"Kuumba, you made a statement at one point. Something to the effect that Zena left you with the feeling that a part was missing from somewhere. Did you have this kind of feeling about her, that she was a heartbreaker?"

Kuumba stared at the lush green jungles beneath them. "No, I had no idea she as a heartbreaker. I felt something else."

"What was it?"

"I felt she wasn't revealing enough to us. I mean, there we were, being open about the history of our lives, in a manner of speaking. And she would listen, smile, enjoy our stories but she never revealed anything about herself. That struck me in a strange way."

"Damn! Why didn't I think of that?"

"Well, brotherman," Kuumba spoke drily, "You had your mind on other things."

"She told us a few things, that she had gone to school in California...stuff like that."

"Yeahhh, she gave up some basic stuff, but it didn't say a lot. I never really understood what she was doing in Brazil.

115

I had no real sense of a frame of reference for her. Don't get me wrong, I dug the lady, too. She just had too many missing pieces for my money. When I get into a woman as beautiful as Zena, I wasn't to know where all of her ex-men are positioned, who she gets her inspiration from, what makes her a whole. I just couldn't seem to get that from her."

They had to circle the Ganibon National Airport twice, to give some children herding goats a chance to clear the runway. The fever was creeping back into their lives, the fever to be in different place, doing different things, moving to a different rhythm. They paused at the exit, blasted into place by the furnace heat and spongy humidity.

"Wow, now this is what I call some serious heat."

"I heard that. Man, what is that smell?"

"It's rich, ain't it?"

They walked five hundred yards off the tarmac, to the airport terminal. "Tony, don't think I'm being funny or anything, but that smell is like, it's like sex." Subconsciously they felt that Brazil had been an excellent preparation for Ganibon. There was no matter how badly they were put together. Nothing they had read about the place prepared them for the scene. In the taxi on the way to the Hotel Ganibon, they studied the people, the scene, and exchanged notes from opposite windows.

"Laid back, completely laid back, that's the impression I get."

"Not from this side. Looks like everybody is in a frenzy on this side."

"It could be Harlem, 1930s, with robes and stuff."

Ganibon. Independence fought for, granted by the English in 1966. Population, five million. Capital, Ganibona. Official language, English; Bona and Gani widely spoken. Per capita income $1,500 Ganibenes per year. Major exports, cocoa, coconut oil, sisal, carvings, fish and peanuts. Large mineral

116

resources, untapped. "Democratic" form of government with Socialist fringes."

They had been told about the Hotel Ganibon. "The artistic people hang out at the Ganibon." They were welcomed as though they were old friends. "Ahhh yes, brother Brown and brother Jones, we are honored to have you stay at the Hotel Ganibon, we will do everything to make your stay a pleasant one." They had decided to spend the first month in a hotel and then branch out, either to buy a house or rent one. They were out on the streets of the city within one hour after their arrival, soaking in the atmosphere, feeling the pulse of the people.

"Well, one thing we know for certain is that there are some beautiful ladies in town."

"You won't find me disagreeing with you."

Kuumba studied his friend's face as they paused for lemonades in a sidewalk cafe. Zena seems to have added a harder line to the brother's jawbone.

"Well, Tony, my brother, what do you think?"

"Huh?"

"What do I think?"

"About the scene, about Ganibon?"

Tony swept his eyes up and down the broad, palm tree lined boulevards, taking in the people who were fashionably dressed in the Ganibon style, music of the kora and kutero drums gently pulsating form four different directions.

"I like it, Kuumba, I like it."

They people-watched through another lemonade. They were pleasantly relieved as the heat and humidity cooled into evening. Once again they probed the city's streets, checking things out.

"Man, you know something? I really dig this place."

"Yeah, me to."

They sound of a piano, bass and drums drew them into

the Club Kiki.

"Hmmm, sounds like a little Errol Garner influence on the piano." Tony smiled for the first time since they'd left Brazil, watching Theolonius Seminole Kuumba Brown's fingers twitch. The Club Kiki opened onto a spacious patio, open to the sky, horse shoe shaped. They were surprised to see that a woman was playing the piano.

"Kuumba, check her out, man."

"I am checking her out, check this club out."

The Jones-Brown telepathy had communicated—this is the club we want—before they were seated. Kuumba was recognized and invited to play during the last set. He didn't go to the piano bench reluctantly. He hadn't practiced for many hours and felt the urge to play.

Two hours later they made a triumphant exit form the club, led arm-in-arm, by Carmen Lovangba, the pianist.

"Ahhh, brother Brown...."

"Call me Kuumba, that's what my friends call me."

"Kuumba, you are absolutely the greatest. I have listened to your records many times."

"I've only made nine."

"Yes, I know. And you, brother Jones..."

"Tony to you."

"Tony, I have read all of your books and many others things you have written."

They discovered, over the course of their first week, in the country, that they were not completely unknown. The bookstores carried vintage works by Jones, as well as his more up to date stuff and the music stores had "songs by Brown." They felt at ease with the scene.

"Tony, we gotta have that club. It's perfect."

"I've already spoken to the owner. He doesn't really want to sell but I'm offering him a pinch more each time and I do believe he's softening. It should take a couple more weeks to reel him in."

Tony's prediction/forecast became a reality two long weeks later.

"How did you convince him to sell?"

"The usual way, brother man, the usual way. I appealed to his sense of greed."

"Well, we're over. Are we still going to call the place Zena's?" Kuumba could tell he had made a boo-boo from the pained expression on his friend's face.

"I don't think it would be a good idea to call our successful jazz club Zena. As a matter of fact, I don't think it would be a good idea to mention than woman's name in presence again, ever."

The Jazz Place opened after three months of intensive redecoration and Tony Nia Jones's Jones' PR. They were determined to reach for every level of Ganibon society. The President, Nat Vesey Ga, came on opening night and offered his blessings. The Jazz Place was declared a success in the second month of operation.

"Looks like we've done it, brother, looks like we got a goodie on our hands."

They opened up their stage to the musical talents of Ganibon.

"Man, did you hear the guitar that young blood was playing?"

"How about the sister?"

"The one who sounded like Aretha?"

"Oh, she was bad, too. I'm thinking about the one who sounds like Sarah Vaughn."

"Yes, Lawd! And she was kinda cute, too, wasn't she?"

They were an established hit after six months. Jazz musicians from America and aficionados from all over made their way to the Jazz Place. Tony and Kuumba ran a tight, happy ship. They gave newcomers an opportunity and offered a venue for respected elders. Kuumba played at least once a week, usually on Saturday. They were the "in" crowd. They were young, handsome, articulate, talented, hot. Kuumba casually rolled with the flow.

"Tony, why don't you make this afternoon tea set with me, man? Bound to be a heap of interesting ladies there."

"Kuumba, I think I've met as many interesting ladies as I'd care to meet for one year, thank you"

"Hey, just thought I'd check." Kuumba could see the hurt but didn't know what to do about it. He felt confident that his friend would get past his heartbreak, but in the interim he felt echoes of the pain he saw in Tony's face.

They had reached the mellow point of being able to talk about what had happened at the end of the business day.

"Kuumba, you've got to explain this to me, man. Explain why she strung me out the way she did."

"Hey, Tony, like my daddy used to say, no one can really say why women behave the way they do."

"That sounds like a proverb, man. I need an explanation. Are you hip to the fact that I committed myself to this woman? I was going to marry her, have kids with her, settle down," if that's what she wanted. And what did she do? She hung me out to dry."

Weeks would pass sometimes before Tony's love would come down on him, but when it did, it fell like a ton of bricks. Kuumba, Numbah One Friend, tried to figure out ways to re-channel the love-grief.

"Tony, I got an idea, man, why don't we go fishin', get away for a few days?"

"Whose going to look after the saloon while we're gone?"

"Well, Carman is just about as efficient as a club manager can get."

"Naww, you go. I'll stay here and drink."

"Heyyyy, you better cool it with that firewater, pal, its

been known to cause headaches." Tony scoffed at the notion that he would ever become a victim of "firewater," but a week later, after he had lined three fifths of cognac up and downed them in succession, he had a little talk with himself in the bathroom mirror.

"Awright, brother Jones, that's enough boozin' for you."

Kuumba took note of a couple more hard lines that had settled into the corners of his friend's mouth, the odd way he refused to allow the beautiful sisters of Ganibon to get close to him.

"Tony, are you trying to go celibate up in here?"

"Who's being celibate? I go over to Momma Cha Cha's place about every two weeks."

"But that's purely a commercial outlet, you can't get no real loving there."

"I get what I need and I don't get my heart broken in the process." Kuumba let it slide, not feeling qualified to put himself in another man's skin.

The Jazz Place became a featured sector of the capital; deals were made and unmade there, murders and *coup d'etats* planed, international reputations made and unmade. Tony seemed to be almost indifferent to the success of the establishment, which made him the focus of a number of romantic intentions. Women of all colors and nationalities gravitated toward the cold, handsome African-American who only appeared to be interested in bringing avant garde jazz to Ganibon. They were intrigued by his coldness. A number of them made an effort to play on his friendship with Kuumba.

"Mr. Brown, would you ask Mr. Jones to join us?"

"Sorry, princess, Mr. Jones never fraternizes with the customers."

Kuumba made his own appeals."'Uhhh, Tony, my brother, I don't want you to get me wrong or anything but I feel I

121

have to say this.''

"Spit it out, man, you know we don't have any fences between us.''

"Well, it concerns that woman you're carrying the torch for . . .''

"You're talking about Zena.''

"Yeah, I'm talking about Zena.''

"I don't wanna talk about her, man.''

"That's what I mean, I think we oughta talk about her.''

"Why?''

"Why not? It's been almost a year now, time to re-new the skin shuffle off into some new sunsets, do another do. It ain't healthy to brood on somebody for too long.''

"Kuumba, I can dig where you're comin' from, but you don't seem to understand, I'm haunted by this woman.''

"You're haunted?''

"Yeah, haunted. Sounds weird, huh?'' He tried, but couldn't explain the magic of what had happened in Brazil, the fragrant nights in the samba clubs, the dawns on the copacabana, the twilight love scenes, the betrayal.

The Jazz Place was a hit, that was the important thing. The club was making people aware of Africa's American classical music and turning a profit. In addition, Tony "Nia" Jones captured the writing laurels with his coldblooded assessment of life in the so-called "Third World.'' They were "hot'' and reaping the benefits of their move to Ganibon.

President Ga offered them special considerations because of he loved jazz music and he was an ardent fan of Tony Jones' work.

"Man, could you imagine anything like this happenin' in the States? The President checking us out personally?'' They enjoyed the privileges it gave them. A sense of freedom that they'd never had before. They worked hard, played hard and tried to give as much back to Ganibon as it was giving to them. Kuumba fell in love with four of Ganibon's most beautiful women watching Tony square away from a similar fate. The first successful year fed into the spring of the second year. And suddenly, lighting struck. Kuumba felt the hair on the back of this neck bristle up when he saw her glide in. His funk ridden reading of "Night in Tunisia" suddenly wandered into patches of Alban Berg and John Cage.

Damn! Where in the fuck did she come from?

They locked eyes in the dim light, midway into his pianistic collage; she seemed to be surprised as he was. Kuumba looked anxiously up to the upstairs office, praying that he could get rid of Zena the heartbreaker before Tony finished checking the books and came down. He sent the ensemble (Ganibon congas, upright bass, Ganibon upcountry flute, chekere and Ganibon talking drum) off onto an extended version of the moment and circumnavigated the club to get to her table. The ensemble could hold them off at the pass, easily, for ten minutes.

"What the fuck are you doing here?" he whispered fiercely into her ear.

"I can't answer that. What're you doing here?"

"We own the joint."

Tony, tripping down the steps from the club office, recounting salaries, liquor import costs, the heat of five Ganibon deals in his head, almost dismissed the vision of the woman talking in urgent whispers to Kuumba. He realized who she was from her gestures. Zena. He grabbed the handrails, stunned as though he had been shot, and practically staggered over to their table. Zena, meanwhile, was trying to make Kuumba understand why she hadn't kept her appointment to come to Africa with Tony.

"Kuumba, I had no choice. Let me please make you understand that. My life is a lot more complicated than it seems."

123

"Do you realize you almost destroyed my friend?"

"I'll never be able to apologize for the hurt I caused him, I know that."

"I believe you. There is something you can do right now, though, you can get up right now and leave."

Tony stood in front of them, feeling drained. He checked off conflicting thoughts. I'm going to disgrace myself and jump on this woman, right in the middle of the Jazz Place. The urge to strangle, kick, punch, mutilate, surrendered to a brutal cool. Kuumba watched the metamorphosis, enthralled. Tony made a slight, sarcastic bow.

"Good evening, Zena, welcome to the Jazz Place."

Kuumba backed away to his piano, settling the ensemble into the homestretch of "Night in Tunisia." He felt out of it and made it plain with the musical declaration of independence.

Fuck y'all, both of you complicated bastards, fight it out as best you can. He plunged the ensemble back into deep waters with a rhapsodic version of *Anabaecoa*.

Zena looked into Tony's face, determined to be as honest as possible. "Tony, please sit down, I know you want me to explain what happened, why I didn't meet you. You deserve an explanation..."

He remained standing, attracting attention to their conversation, seething. "No, I don't want any of that. I just want you to know that whatever you want is on the house, my treat." He stiffly moved away from her table, faking smiles to the regulars, almost blinded by new tears and the pounding at his temples.

She returned two nights later, mint green, beige and saffron ganibobo draped around her body. Tony stared a hole through her head and made a suave disappearance up the stairs to his office. His cool-hip-composure crumbled the minute he closed the office door.

If she had been a mirage the first night, a real figment of this madness, it was co-signed by her reappearance. Zena was here, in Ganibon, in their club. He poured himself a large cognac and slopped down on the sofa, stared out of the picture window at the midnight shape of Ganibon. The tears surprised him. He wiped his hands across his eyes, started at the salty droplets. In the darkened room, his hands cradling the cognac snifter, he subconsciously, torturously, recreated their scene, the samba ridden midnights that led to dawn-streaked love feasts, the crystal magic of Rio at high noon, the pulse they shared.

Ganibon seemed to sizzle in front of him, whole sections blazed red, counterpointed by blue or green and yellow, electric, in motion. Ganibon was a Brazilian facet, a diamond in retrospect. He sipped his cognac and allowed the tears to flow down his cheeks. He felt melancholic, blue, almost suicidal.

The soft tapping at the door seemed almost natural, a part of his feeling. "Come in, it's open," he called out and twisted reminders at his head.

"Tony, can I talk to you?"

He felt the sudden, irrational urge to leap at her, to kill her.

"Yes, yes, you can talk to me...come on in." He was enchanted by the shimmering silks that enveloped her. The national garment of the women of Ganibon, officially called the gaboni, was a perfect garment for Zena. She drifted over to him, silks glistening and switching in the dimly lit room, her perfume, so subtle that it seemed like an afterthought, and eased into the space beside him. He flinched involuntarily, overwhelmed by her presence.

"Tony, please don't. Please let me explain." He felt vaguely malicious, unreasonable.

"Why should I let you explain anything to me"

"Because," she answered without hesitation, "because

125

you're in love with me and I think I love you too." He canceled the urge to throw his drink in her face.

"You *think* you love me too...? In Rio you told me that you loved me, you told me that you wanted to live the rest of your life with me. You didn't say anything about 'I *think*.' What brought about the change?" He wasn't emotionally prepared to have her slump down beside him on the sofa, tears streaming down her cheeks. He weakened for a moment, stunned by the obvious sincerity of her tears, but immediately recovered, instantly recalling the hurt he felt when she left him stranded at the airport.

"Zena, I think you should to dry your eyes, I'm not turned on by women who shed crocodile tears." She stared at him, her anger turning to compassion, she saw that he had been crying too.

"Tony, I'm not trying to impress you," she said quietly. They avoided looking at each other, awkwardly for a few pregnant moments.

"Can I get you a drink?" She nodded numbly, yes, and stared out at the lights of the capital. He poured her a drink of cognac and sat a little closer to her on the sofa, trying to ignore the fragrance of her perfume. My mother always taught me that there was only one perfume and it was Chanel No. 5,' she once told him in Rio.

"Tony, what do you want me to say to you?"

"Here's lookin' at you, kid," he mimicked Humphrey Bogart's *Casablanca* lines, and sipped his drink, feeling steadier, more in control of himself. The muted sounds of the club floated up to them.

"Please," a breathless, begging tone slipped into her voice, "Please, Tony, let me explain what happened." He felt himself sinking. She was more beautiful than she had been in Rio, darker, more mature.

"Zena, look, you weren't there when we were scheduled

126

to go and I haven't laid eyes on you 'til the other night. I don't think you owe me an explanation. You owe me some cement to paste my fucking heart back together. Is your explanation going to cover that?!'' He watched her eyes begin to glisten with tears, felt the urge to pull her into his arms and whisper, 'everything is cool now, baby, you're here and that's all that matters.'

"Tony, I can't offer you any excuses. I'm not good at that. I can only give you an explanation.'' He stood, swaying a bit from the effect of the cognac and his emotional state, strolled over to the bar and tipped another slug into his glass.

"Zena, you know something, my father warned me about women like you. He told me that one day I would get to know what the blues was all about that a beautiful, treacherous lyin' ass hypocrite would be the cause.''

She shook her head sadly, placed her glass on the cocktail table in front of her and stood up to leave. She had taken three steps toward the door before he grabbed her and crushed her in his arms. He kissed her roughly, bruising his lips on hers. He opened his eyes after a few wild moments, to find her eyes frightened and wide, her arms cinched around his shoulders. They stared at each other as if they were strangers.

"Zena, your really hurt me, baby, you hurt me in a way that I'd never been hurt before.''

"I know,'' she answered, quietly, smothering her face in his chest. A wordless ballet found them slowly unbuttoning buttons, unzipping sippers, uncovering each other. Naked, he led her back to the sofa.

"Tony, Tony,'' she whispered, the lights of Ganibon highlighting their nakedness, "Tony, do you think we should do this?''

"Yes,'' he answered, as they slowly sank down on the sofa.

127

They gazed at the sun sprouting up, meditatively sipping breakfast snifters of cognac, half lotused on the rug in front of the picture window.

"Tony, please, will you please allow me to give you my explanation?" Tony was feeling ambivalent. He had surrendered to a romantic-lustful impulse, and now, at the dawn of a new day, he was beginning to recall the hurt again. He studied her face, traced the wonderful slope of her breasts, the strongly muscled stomach, the indentation of the waist, the flaring hips, the grizzled sporan between her thighs. She was gorgeous and totally unselfconscious in her nakedness. I wonder how many other men she's been naked with . . .

"Go on," he urged, "explain, if you want to."

"I want to explain because I feel I owe you that."

He felt a bitter taste well up in his throat, sucked it down. "Go on, explain. I'll listen."

The sun was halfway up now, yellow bright, hot. She sipped her cognac as though she were preparing to be executed. "First, I have to tell you that I'm married."

He dribbled a little of his drink down his chin in surprise. "You're what?!"

She continued calmly, the sun glistening on her skin. "I was married when we were together in Rio." He frowned involuntarily, midway between disgust and anger. She watched the emotional play race across his face. "You said you'd let me explain." She paused to let it sink in.

"Okay, okay, go on, let's hear this . . ."

"My husband is Marcus Tambolu." Tony lifted his glass for a long, slow sip. Marcus Tambolu, a ranking member of the African National Congress for many years, the official spokesman for the organization. He tried to make his question sound as mean as possible.

"Tambolu is an old man now, isn't he?"

"Yes."

128

"Look, lets get down to cases here, you're telling me that you're married to this old man, that you were married to him when we met. What's the deal?"

"Tony, patience is a virtue, isn't that what you used to tell me?" He was forced to smile, conceding a point.

"I'll make it as brief as possible. My parents have been active in the South African freedom struggle for many years, my dad was a colonel in Vietnam. He specialized in guerrilla warfare training and put his expertise at the disposal of the ANC. I met Marcus through them, mom and dad. I guess, in some ways, it's a familiar story; idealistic young woman, just out of college, looking for a cause, falls in love with an older man, a father figure in many ways,"

"That simple, uh?"

"Tony, don't be cynical, I'm trying to be honest with you."

"Why weren't you completely "honest" with me in Rio?"

"I wanted to Tony, please believe me. I wanted to but I just couldn't spoil what we had." He felt tempted to slap her face, let her know how mixed up and crazy he felt about her. "Marcus had left me in Brazil for two weeks when we met, waiting for him to return. Prior to that, two weeks in Cuba and prior to that..."

"I get the picture, you've spent a to to time waiting for your husband. Didn't you know that you were going to have that kind of life when you got married?"

"Frankly, no, I didn't. I thought I was going to travel, become involved in international intrigue, do a little spying, play a role. Instead, I've found myself being stashed in expensive hotels and some not so expensive, while my husband tripped off to do his thing."

"I don't know if I clearly understand this. Your husband is a major league wheeler dealer in the ANC, you're his beautiful young wife and all you do is just wait around for

129

him to finish doing whatever he does. I don't get it."

"I've been used, you know, from time to time, to make some people more receptive to ANC programs. You know how receptive some people are when they find themselves face to face with an attractive woman."

"So your husband knows how to use a pretty face. Does he know how to take advantage of any of your other assets?" She frowned for a few moments, undecided as to whether she should continue to make the effort to make him understand.

"Tony, don't do this to me. You know I love you, why do you want to make things more difficult for me?"

"I thought you said that you *thought* you loved me?" She crawled across the space separating them and squeezed herself into his arms. He gently pulled himself out of her arms and stood to close the blinds. It was 7:15 am Ganibon time.

Later that afternoon, they floated down the stairs to the club floor, momentarily satiated with each other. Kuumba was already into his second hour of practice. He stared at them, genuinely surprised.

"Well, well, well, what do we have here?" They occupied a table nearby and sprayed angelic smiles in his direction. He returned their smiles as he flickered into slices of Rachamninov, Chopin, Tatum, Berg, Monk and Bud. It had been resolved. She was in Africa, in Ganibon, while her husband swung a deal in Zambia to get more sophisticated arms into the guerrillas who were tearing the tail end of the Apartheid regime to shreds.

"What happens when this dude comes back here and you tell him that you're in love with me and you want a divorce?"

"I don't know that it'll matter all that much. Marcus has always been more married to his work than he was to me." The city of Ganibon suddenly acquired a new charm in

130

Tony's eyes. Although he felt slightly uneasy with Zena, slightly paranoid, he did love her, he knew that. And he chose to be honest about it. The personality change that swept over him made him seem even more attractive to the sisters of Ganibon. He was smiling for the first time since his arrival in the country.

They decided to keep their secret until they'd had a chance to explain the situation to Marcus Tambolu. "When will he return?"

"I don't know, I was expecting him last week. We just have to wait. See what I mean? I was a lonely woman when I met you. A beautiful, lonely woman, the worst kind. We clicked, it was just that simple. Now we're into something serious."

Kuumba tried to pull his coat. "Tony, you must be a glutton for punishment."

"What's that mean?"

"Look brother, I'll say it loud and sharp, that woman is bad news, a downer. What are you trying to do, prove that lightening always strikes twice? I'm not trying to know the sister, you know that. I think it might even be something that she can't control."

Tony stared at the stream of hot sunlight that flooded through the windows of the Jazz Place. He really didn't want to talk to Kuumba. Or anyone. He wanted to see Zena, hold her, feel her warmth, love her, forget the past. He moved away from Kuumba, strolled behind the long bar of the Jazz Place, feeling a sense of pride in their ownership. The Place had beautiful acoustics, excellent sight lines and the hippest clientele in West Africa. He poured two gins and returned to the table, almost determined to fight for his right to have his heart broken again. Kuumba cut him off at the pass.

"You know, it wasn't too much of a problem for everybody in town to know that you were sneakin' around with Tambolu's wife. The drums have been smokin', this is Ganibon, and y'all have been into scandalous behavior. The stuff she's doing could hurt her husband's work. I don't know what you're doing. Do you?''

Tony slumped back in his chair, took a sip of his gin. "What're you saying, Kuumba, what should I do?''

"Step away from the sister, man. That would be the best thing to do.''

"Kuumba, you can't understand this. All you love is your music.''

"I loved that woman in Spain, the dark-eyed one that looked at me in the mirror.'' Tony laughed so hard, he made it contagious. "But I was in love, just as deeply as you love Zena. It doesn't have to take place over decades, pal. It can be as unique as your fingerprints and just as deep. And quick.''

"So that makes you understand even more why she's like a part of me. I don't want to be separated.''

Kuumba sipped his gin. This was going to be harder than he thought. "What're you going to do with her old man when he gets back from Zambia?''

"Damn, you know everything, don't you?''

"It's hard not to know shit this interesting.''

"She's going to get a divorce and we'll get married.''

"What if he doesn't want to give her a divorce. There's a rumor going 'round that says he loves the shit out of her.''

"She'll leave him and we'll be together, period.''

"You got it all figured out, huh?''

"I hope so, man, I really hope so.''

They tripped off to small villages on the outskirts of the capital, they took long walks on the north shore of Lake Kwonba and, once, they were caught making love in the upstairs office of the Jazz Place by one of the cleaning women. Tony began to feel like a man surrounded by

132

circumstances beyond his control. The musical evenings acquired a new significance for their in-group. Kuumba was working/playing through a quartet of concerto length pieces he called "Sketches of Ganibon." Zena and Tony, enchanted by the new music, oblivious to the affectionate stares and the love spiced gossip that raced from table to table.

Carmen Lovangbe, the woman whose piano playing had lured them into the club, played a duet with Kuumba one evening, the first double exposure of the "Sketches of Ganibon" to a receptive public. Kuumba stood at the conclusion of the work and dedicated the piece to "Zena and Tony, two people who are going through a bunch of changes right now."

Two days later Tony had the unmistakable feeling that Marcus Tambolu was back. Two hours later, Zena confirmed it by sending a ten year old messenger to him.

'My husband has returned.' He stared at the note. 'My husband has returned.' What the fuck was that supposed to mean?

"You have a return message, suh?"

"Uhh, no, no return message."

He tipped the messenger a generous five Ganibenes and slumped on his sofa to stare out at the familiar designs of the city.

'My husband has returned.' What kind of position does that put me in? What am I supposed to do, sit here and hold my nuts until further notice? Kuumba popped in on him while he was still in suspended animation.

"Well, well, what do we have here?"

"What's it look like?"

"I'd hate to begin to tell you."

"Don't even try, here, check this out." He handed his friend the message. Kuumba studied the note for a long moment.

133

"Sounds like she's trying to tell you something."

Tony frowned and slumped deeper into the sofa. It didn't make a lot of sense to try to get a fair assessment of the situation from Kuumba, he was already prejudiced about the situation. He decided to chill for a couple days, rest his head, put a program together for him and Zena.

He stared at the empty page in the notebook, trying to decide whether he wanted to begin the second draft of the fifth chapter of "Simone" or go downstairs to do the business of running a night club.

Well, no matter what, the club will be in good hands, whether I go downstairs or not. I'll still have a problem trying to deal with this page. He made a creative decision. I'm gonna stay up here and deal with this...

The knocking on the door startled and annoyed him. Damn. I thought I told them to leave me alone for the next few hours. The short, gray-bearded, distinguished looking African man in the French suit smiled slightly when he opened the door. A larger version of the man shadowed him, obviously a bodyguard.

"Mr. Jones?"

Tony nodded affirmatively, he already knew who his visitor was.

"My name is Marcus Tambolu. May I come in?" Tony made what he felt was a gracious how and motioned for Marcus Tambolu to enter. Well, so much for the fifth chapter this evening. He closed the door and turned to face his visitor.

"Mr. Tambolu, seems like I've been reading quite a bit about you lately."

"Mostly lies, no doubt."

Tony took Tambolu's measure; he was obviously in his sixties but he gave the impression of being strong, in the way that a tree grows stronger as it ages. "Please be seated, Mr. Tambolu, can I make you a drink?"

"A glass of water would be fine, thank you."

Tony strolled over to pour water from his water container and to pour himself a neat shot of Beefeater. Hummm, this ought to be interesting. "Your water, sir."

They touched glass rims like old friends and looked into each others faces, they felt open to each other.

"Mr. Jones?"

"Call me Tony, please."

"And you must call me Marcus."

Tony was tempted to laugh at the formality of it all. They made small, subconscious bows to each other, to demonstrate respect. They sipped, trying to find the right rhythm and tone for things.

"Well, let's get to it, you came here to talk to me about your wife, about Zena, and I think it's a good idea. Let's talk."

Tambolu smiled a sad little smile. "There's really nothing to talk about, my wife loves you and wants to be with you. There's nothing I can do about that. It's a 'done deal,' as you say in America."

Tony felt guarded, alert for the old man's tricks; he must have some, working for the ANC. He felt trapped by the old man's calmness.

"Seems like you're saying you won't try to prevent us from being together?"

"I have to tell you what I told Zena. I told her that I love her with all of the strength of my heart, but I love our people more. I told her, 'You will leave me, my wife, a great source of spiritual comfort, to go off and have sex with another man. It isn't fair to our people that you should give yourself so cheaply.'"

Tony sipped his drink. Soooo, this is the way its played in the Big Leagues. After all, Marcus Tambolu had hung out with Castro, Arafat and Ortega. He's going to try to make me feel guilty for stealing his "spiritual comfort" away.

"What about me, Marcus, don't I need some spiritual comfort, too?"

"I don't think that concerns you as much. You are not trying to gain freedom for millions of our people. I'm not saying that you're not a good person, but you must understand what it is to have a woman who only knows one love and that is you alone."

"But she doesn't love you alone anymore, she loves me, we love each other."

"Zena doesn't know what she wants and I think you are too wrapped up in your personal desires to relate to a larger cause. May I have a bit more water, please?" Tony automatically reached for his glass. He felt as though he were being manipulated by someone with superior logic. *What do I really want from this woman, other than to make love to her often as I can? That'll take us through a wonderful two years and then we'll go to another plane, but we definitely wouldn't be helping to free millions of people.*

Tony handed him a fresh glass of water, feeling shaky. "You really love Zena, don't you?"

Tambolu's face glowed as he struggled to describe how much he loved her. "I would die without her."

The noises from the club begin to filter in. "So, in effect, you are asking me to back away from Zena, because of the effect it would have on the Liberation struggle?"

Tambolu's face lost its gloss, hardened, his eyes slitted. "I could have had you killed. Are you aware of that?" A shiver died halfway up Tony's back. *No time to chicken out now.*

"You wouldn't do that. I couldn't imagine you asking your people to do something that personal."

"That's exactly what I'm trying to get you to see, Jones. You're merely thinking of your own personal desires and urges, while I'm thinking of a greater cause. You simply want a woman, I want a soul near me, a special kind of soul. Zena has that for me, she is spiritually attached to me. We have a great work to accomplish.''

Tony drained his short glass, pissed at the nerve of the man. ''Look Marcus what would you do if you were in my situation?''

The answer slammed him in the head.

''I would give the woman up for the greater cause and go away.'' Tony frowned at his own dumb question. What did you expect him to say? The two men stared into each other's faces for a hard minute. ''Marcus, you drive a hard bargain, you know that?''

''And a fair bargain.''

''Well, that remains to be seen.''

''It all depends on whose looking at it.''

Once again they exchanged opaque looks.

''One more question. what kind of time frame are we looking at here?''

Once again, Marcus Tambolu caught Tony slightly off balance with his rapid fire reply. ''Within two weeks, at the end of this month, I'll be leaving Ganibon. I hope and pray that Zena will be with me when I leave.''

''Aren't we forgetting someone here. What about Zena? Shouldn't she be the one to make this decision?''

''No, Zena is a young woman, she is ruled by emotions and passions. We are men, we must make the right decision for her.''

Tony strolled behind Marcus Tambolu, tempted to hit him in the head with something. Tambolu turned to him as he opened the door, ushering in the club noises, smiled his sad little smile.

''You have a nice place here, Tony Jones.''

''Yeahhh, we like to think so.''

137

And then he was gone.

They occupied their table, sipping spring water and monitoring the intermission crowd. Phavia Kujichagulia was good for the house, for as long as she chose to stay, which was never too long because her talents were in demand everywhere. Her next stop was Rio. But for now, she was playing a week at the Jazz Place, giving the audiences a superior mix of vocal and instrumental music, coupled to a poetry that was so hip that it was still being understood. She was also so fine that she made Tony feel tempted to think lascivious thoughts about her.

"So what're you planning to do? Have you talked to Zena?"

"I haven't been able to reach her since the day she sent the message over, you know, when she wrote, 'my husband has returned.'"

Pleased patrons smiled their way past the owners' table, Tony and Kuumba responded with a nod here, a smile there, a handshake.

"Tony, Tony, my brother, my brother, what does it take for you to learn your lesson? The sister was fascinated with you for a minute, her man was off taking care of business. He's back now, he wants her and he needs her, 'cording to what you say, and that seems to be the way it's gonna be."

Zena appeared with the flow of people coming in for the last set Tony felt blood rush to his head, a funny feeling turn over in his stomach. She was here and they were going to be together, he knew it.

Kuumba watched her slither toward their table, Ganibon's finest silks curled around her body, tossed over her shoulder in high Ganibon fashion. The ganibobo was made for her.

"Here, lovely lady, take my chair. I've got to check back stage to make certain everything is working the way it's supposed to be. Sister Phavia demands that everything should be working the way it's supposed to be and I'm one hundred percent in her corner. Tony, we'll rap later.'' Kuumba made a point of giving Zena a slow, cynical once over, before moving away.

"Tony, I don't think your friend likes me."

"How do you know I like you? I haven't heard from you in a week." The sudden image of "his" Zena, sprawled in bed next to Marcus Tambolu, suddenly made him angry, jealous.

"Tony," she pleaded, "I couldn't see you until now, I just couldn't."

"But now it's cool, huh?"

"Well, yes, in a way. I had to come see Phavia. We lived in the same hotel in Spain last year. We became friends."

"What about me, Zena? What about me? I've been waiting to hear from you, to find out what's going to happen with us? Are we still going to be together or what?"

She answered in a shaky voice. "Tony, we have to talk about this."

The magic of Phavia Kujichagulia's opening song with chekere cooled out his urge to get loud and disorderly. He gestured for her to follow him upstairs. "Wait five minutes," he whispered across the table. He tripped up the stairs, opened the door, closed it and immediately slumped on the sofa. Damn! What's happening to me?! I'm behaving like a lovesick chump. He felt the urge to have a neat gin but decided against it. No need to clutter up my feeling with ignunt oil. I'm already feeling a little crazy as it is.

Eight minutes elapsed before he heard a soft knock on the door. He left like screaming, 'what the hell took you so long?' "Come in, come in, the door is open."

Zena slid into the room past a patch of light, the sound of Kujichagulia's trumpet echoing in the background. Tony stood and held his arms out for her. They locked themselves

139

into each other's embrace and swayed from side to side.

"Tony, I missed you so much."

He was speechless, numb with emotions.

"I think about you all the time."

"You do?" he asked, trying to sound sarcastic.

"Yes, all the time."

He felt as though he wanted to swallow her with kisses, communicated everything through his feeling. Minutes passed before they were able to pull themselves apart. Tony made an effort to recall his agenda. "Zena, come over here and sit beside me on the sofa, we have to talk about our future." He was startled to see the quick look of panic grip her face. They sat on the sofa's edge, staring anxiously at each other.

"Zena, what's wrong, baby? You look disturbed about something."

"I'm not really disturbed, as you put it. I just feel a little disturbed about us."

"About us?"

"Yes, it's so important for us to make the right decision."

"Right or wrong, my decision was made months ago, in Rio. I made a decision that we were going to start a life together. I don't care whether we get married or live together or what. I just know I love you and I want to share my life with you." He was shook by her sudden burst of tears.

"Tony, it's not that simple. I wish it were."

"What's the problem, baby, don't you love me anymore?" The short burst of tears became a flood.

"I do love you but I also love what my husband is doing."

Tony strolled slowly to the bar. The situation was making him uncomfortable. She nodded 'no' to his offer of a cognac. No peace offerings tonight. "You love what your husband is doing? Sounds like you're trying to tell me something."

"Tony, please, don't you understand? I love you but we're

just two people who want to share a good time. Marcus is trying to do something a lot greater than that.''

"Uhh ooooh, sounds like we're approaching familiar ground. Kuumba told me there would be days like this. So, let's have it straight up, you love me but you can't leave Marcus because it would hurt too many people. Or something like that.''

"I *could* leave him, if you were willing to take the responsibility for whatever might happen.''

"And what do you think might happen.''

"I think my leaving him would kill him.''

"Hmmmmm...that sounds like familiar ground, too.''

"I'm simply telling you that I know what will happen to him, if I leave him. I want to be with you. I love you, don't you understand?'' She melted into his arms, reviving the fix they took from each other. Three hours later, they stood at the curb in front of the Jazz Place, waiting for a taxi.

"Zena, I want you to take a week to think this out. When you come to me, I want you to be certain that you're with me one hundred percent.''

"That's the way I'd like to have it, too.''

They kissed one last time, delaying the cab for five minutes, and then, suddenly, she was gone, wrapped up by the chic boulevards of Ganibon.

"What's happenin' with you, man? You act like somebody without a woman.''

"Don't joke with me like that, Kuumba, you know how that goes through me.''

"Sorry, man, just playing, but the fact is that you don't have a woman.''

"You can't say that.''

"Wasn't she supposed to be leaving her husband for you at the end of last week.''

"She was going to make a decision.''

141

"But wasn't she supposed to do that last week?"

"My guess is that she got hung up, busy doing something else."

"If you want my plain-spoken opinion, I think you've been had again. You never will learn, will you?"

The agony of the days and nights waiting, waiting for a message, or a phone call, a letter, had worn Tony down. He had lost eight pounds and had dark circles under his eyes. He didn't feel up to arguing with anybody.

The phone call came later that evening, at the beginning of Kuumba's first set. "Tony," she whispered into his ear, "forgive me for taking so long to get back to you, but I couldn't talk to you before now."

He was saved, she was calling, nothing else mattered.

"Don't think about it, it's behind us . . ." He felt a rush of air through the receiver, like the suction of a blast from a bomb.

"Tony, I can't come to you. I must stay with Marcus."

He felt like dropping to his knees and begging but he stiffened up. Don't make a fool of yourself.

"That's your final word?"

"Yes."

He heard a steel plated sound in her 'yes.' That's it, the woman I dreamed about is gone. Returned. Fled.

"Good luck to you, Zena, and to Marcus, too."

"We knew you would understand."

"They always say that, Zena, it's been in a thousand "B" movies."

"Tony, I'm so sorry, I love you so much, but I feel I must make this sacrifice."

"Take it easy, Zena, see you around."

Kuumba finished up his last set and made his way to the bar for a Perrier and lime, satisfied with the reception of his two new pieces. What the hell happened to Tony? He would've dug the last set. Kuumba was creating a four part work called "Sketches of Ganibon" and played sections of it each weekend. Wonder where the dude is? He smiled and nodded his way through the turned on audience. He knocked on the office door, a courtesy they extended to each other because both of them had been caught at least twice.

Tony stood in front of the picture window, tears streaming down his face. Kuumba paused at the bar to have a glass of mineral water. What the hell could you say to man who was hurting the way his friend was hurting?

"Been stood up again, pal, that why you're why you're crying like a baby?"

Kuumba almost made Tony laugh at the absurdity of the whole thing. Kuumba had struck the right chord.

"Yeah, that's the way it looks, doesn't it?"

"Ain't no need for you to be crying, you've had enough experience being stood up, you ought to be used to it by now."

Tony embraced him, Kuumba didn't believe in excessive sentimentality unless it involved him directly.

"C'mon, man, let's go downstairs and be cordial to the masses. I've been stood up again, I oughta be able to carry on big time fun with your philosophy to back me up."

"Win some, lose some, I always say."

Three months later, Tony became aware that he was going to become a father.

"Kuumba, I'm going to become a father!"

"Oh really, who's the lucky woman?"

"Zena."

Kuumba held his head in his hands and moaned. "O lawd, please hep dis boy, he done pure idee lost his mind. You mean, after all the times this woman has left you, stood you up or whatever, she's got the nerve to tell you that you're the father of her unborn child? You believe that?"

143

"I believe it. Here, check this out. She sent me this from Mozambique. Read it out loud."

Kuumba felt vaguely irritated by the whole thing. The woman was obviously full of shit and he couldn't make himself believe that Tony would fall for the big trick: I'm pregnant.

"'Dear Tony, I hope you are well and continuing to enjoy a creative life. We are in Mozambique for a conference and something big is about to happen. I know you will be surprised to receive this note. I felt compelled to write you, to let you know that I'm going to have our baby.'"

Kuumba yawned, trying to stifle a belly laugh "Damn, she get's right into things doesn't she?'"

"The plot thickens, read on."

"'Marcus thinks the child is his and I won't tell him the truth, if you agree...'She wants the whole coconut, huh? She gets a chance to love on you a little but run off with her husband and have your baby. She's good, bro', real good. And everybody lives happily ever after."

Tony snatched the letter from his friend's hands.

"I'm gon' raise hell! My child is going to know me."

"But it's not your child, legally, and you sure as hell won't be having Zena filing paternity charges on you. And how do you know it's yours anyway?"

He didn't feel the need to act, hesitate.

"I know it's mine, Kuumba. Remember the night Phavia Kujichagulia played here?" Kuumba pursed his lips, remembering.

"I think a few people will always remember."

They enlarged the main room of the Jazz Place. Kuumba 'discovered' an instrument in an up country village. "Check this out, man. It looks like a Berimbau, but it makes this other kind of sound."

144

Tony was being forced to make a decision for himself and his friend by Marcus Tambolu.

"The need for a revolution very often overshadows personalities, and wants and urges. We must think about what it is our people need, they've been without so much for so long. Are you and your friend willing to help? You could offer us an invaluable source of intelligence. You don't love me, you love my wife, but my wife loves liberation more than either of us, thank the Orisa. Why don't you join us, in the same light of Orisa, that spirit? We need you and Kuumba. You are treasures for us. Put the emotions on hold until the struggle is over."

Tony felt almost sick under the pressure of the old man's pressures. They'd always had the best, him and his partner, never considered the possibility of being shot at and now here was this man talking about making real sacrifices, shit!

He and Kuumba discussed it at length, over coffee, for days. "Yeah, it seems right, if we were at home, we wouldn't be Spike Lee's, we'd be Phavia Kujichagulia's."

"So you think it would be hip to get off into this, huh?"

"Tony, it's a new adventure, shit. How many of us creative people get a chance to get out there and offer solutions to a lot of these crazy ass things that are happening. I truly dig the idea. Can you handle it?"

He felt he could. If Zena could level herself with him in the way she had done, then, why not? And it was for a good cause. Who doesn't like to be a hero? They made plans to sell the Jazz Place, move in closer to the enemy, go to Zimbabwe, open up a Jazz Zimbabwe. Kuumba loved the idea of the move. It meant his friend had regrouped.

"We can make the club the center of operations for whatever we get into and still have a good time."

The week before their move, Tony received his second note from Zena. 'We have just returned from an exhausting trip to Angola. Our son was born July 6th and he is a really remarkable three month old. We call him Marcus Tambolu, the second.'

Kuumba accepted his *Romeo y Julieta* with a cynical remark. ''First time I've ever been give a cigar to celebrate the birth of another man's child, by the man that the child is supposed to be by...''

''Kuumba, that's not going to make me feel bad. Marcus Tambolu II doesn't sound *too* terrible, does it?''

The Jazz Place was immediately snatched off the market by the President's nephew. ''Kuumba, Tony, I can't tell you how much we appreciate what you've done for the capital, for our country. I hope I can continue the great jazz tradition you have started here.''

They took the money and eased into Zimbabwe. Bulawayo was almost the exact opposite of Ganibon. The weather was hot but dry, the people almost conservative, the atmosphere tense with anticipation of another South African guerrilla assault.

''You must understand, my friends, many people are leaving because they fear the bully boy of our region. We have all finally come to the realization that the South African government does not want a peaceful solution. They want to fight until it is no longer profitable. The Portuguese and others who fled to South Africa after Mozambique was recovered, are now fleeing South Africa because they remember what happened in Mozambique. In addition, there are a number of whites who fled 'Rhodesia' when it became Zimbabwe, who are once again fleeing. They recognize the stupidity of trying to keep the African people of South Africa in slavery.''

It took them three months to find the Jazz Zimbabwe Club and their efforts were not blessed by the Bulawayo City Council.

146

"Gent'men, you both seem to be intelligent men, why waste your money on a jazz club?" The stiff headed African of British persuasion was not someone who loved or understood African-American music. He thought Charlie Parker and Rahsaan Roland Kirk were the names of white rock groups and had never heard of ragtime.

Kuumba diplomatically re-educated him for thirty minutes before they were granted the license to open Jazz Zimbabwe.

"Wowwww! You believe that dude, man?!"

"I wouldn't've if I hadn't seen and heard him."

The meeting that they had with the local ANC representative was much more cordial. "Brothers, welcome to Zimbabwe, and welcome to the struggle to free South Africa from the claws of the beast."

Tony felt like he was bumping into the shadow off Marcus Tambolu wherever he turned, it almost seemed that Tambolu was the ANC.

"We must wait for brother Tambolu's return before we can discuss your application for membership in our organization."

"We are not asking to be full fledged members, we just want to do what we can to help the struggle end."

They set about the business of making the Jazz Zimbabwe Club into a Jazz Place. It wasn't difficult. The room seated one hundred comfortably and they made it expensive. They had decided to go for the well to do and pass the goodies along to the ANC.

"Marvelous show, Kuumba, marvelous show. We haven't heard such music since our last trip to New Yawk City. Congratulations."

Tony played the opaque intellectual, Kuumba, the esoteric musician. They became a refuge for guerrilla fighters being shuttled back into South Africa from Libya, Algiers, Stockholm, the Soviet Union, Cuba, Iran and Ganibon.

"Ganibon is in on it? I didn't know that!"

"We should've known that they were in on things, they're super people, I'd like to trip back to Ganibon someday."

"Yeah, me too."

The sight of Marcus Tambolu striding up the center aisle of the deserted club at midday seemed almost natural. Tony welcomed the visitor with a touch of sarcasm. "Mr. Tambolu, I presume?"

They smiled into each other's faces, almost liking each other, in spite of the circumstances that bound them. "Welcome to Zimbabwe, Tony Jones. I'm very pleased that you and your friend made the right decision." Tony felt charmed by the man's manner. He gave the impression of being humble, almost too gentle to be a warrior. Maybe it's all an act.

Tony sent one of the cleaning people for Kuumba. They sat at a table in the dining room, nursing cups of tea, waiting for Kuumba.

"Mr. Jones?"

"Marcus, call me Tony, okay?"

"Okay, Tony. I have exactly half an hour to say all that has to be said..."

"Kuumba won't be long. He's at the tennis club down the street."

Kuumba tripped in, perspiring from an hour of lazy man's tennis, alert and ready. He admired Tony for being able to sublimate his crazy need for something that really mattered. Marcus Tambolu, the leader, took them in hand, forcefully, gracefully.

"Now then, gentlemen, this is what our organization needs to have done. You are not offered the option of accepting or rejecting any demands that we may impose on you.

"We've found that it's best not to fool around with too many bureaucratic procedures. The Afrikaners put a bad taste in our mouth concerning bureaucracies."

They shook hands as Tambolu stood to signal that the meeting was over. Tony felt puffed up about being in the ANC.

"Uhhh, what are you planning to have us do?" Kuumba asked, as they accompanied their guest to the exit.

Tambolu turned his sad little smile on the two of them, making them feel awed by the humanness of such a powerful person. "Don't worry, we'll let you know what needs to be done. Oh, incidentally, did I mention that I have a new son?"

Tony stiffen'd up. There had to be some reason for him bringing this up.

"No, you didn't mention it," Kuumba answered with a straight face.

"Would you like to see a picture of him?" He directed the question at Tony. Tony nodded yes, feeling numb. What a helluva position to be caught in. Tony stared at the picture, filling his eyes up with a six month old version of his own face.

"Beautiful child, isn't he?"

"Yes, yes, he is."

Kuumba added "congratulations" in a very dry voice. Tony frowned, trying to wipe his head clear of the image of Zena.

"I think that congratulations are in order for you, Mr. Jones."

Tony's frown widened. "I don't think I understand."

"I think you do. I'm sure I don't have to tell Zena this, she already knows. I haven't been potent since the South African secret police tortured me, back in 1987."

They shook hands once more as he exited, suddenly surrounded by bodyguards. Tony and Kuumba stood at the curb, watching Tambolu and his bodyguards pull away.

"Tony, you know something, man? That dude is deep."

"Hey, tell me about it."

Later that night, Tony sprawled across his bed, a snifter of Arc d' Triumph beside the bed, John Coltrane's "Lush Life" filling up the air, his mind wandering from the picture that Marcus Tambolu had shown them.

My son...

Zena...

The ANC...

He sipped his cognac, trying to push the thought of Zena out of his mind. The harder he tried, the more she intruded. It was such a crazy situation. He sat up on the side of the bed, wishing that he were in another lace in the work. Why in the hell am I here? Why is she here? Marcus Tambolu II. He started crying. The impotent anger that he felt about having his life governed by forces beyond his control caused him to squeeze tears through clenched eyelids. He wanted to smash something, scream, wake up from the nightmare.

The moments passed and he sprawled back again, relaxing, allowing himself to become the filter for whatever came to his head. I wish I had Tambolu's focus. Here's a man who could be torn to bits by a bomb, by an emotion, by the elements that would like to see him dead. And yet, he's cool. I need to be cool like that.

Zena, Zena, Zena, why did you have to come into my life? Why?

Jazz Zimbabwe caught on slowly and definitely. Tony worked on a new novel he called "The Afrikaner Conspiracy," exploring the possibility that the South African regime might be distributing crack cocaine in the Bantustans of North America. Kuumba finished "Sketches of Ganibon." They waited impatiently to be told/asked when their services would be needed.

Two months ground past before they received the work. "We're sending two white men to you. Their names are

Frank Benson and Sidney Cranston. We want you to help them establish themselves as talent scouts for an American recording company.''

"Who are these guys really?''

"Please, Mr. Jones, no questions.''

It wasn't difficult to palm off the two well fed obviously affluent Americans as record producers. They were in search of home grown talent and Jazz Zimbabwe was the ideal place to find it. The 'producers' came to them after two weeks of monitoring the club's activities and asked them sly questions about Marcus Tambolu and the organization. Tony smelled a rat and got in touch with their contact man, Amos Maskela.

"Brother Maskela, these two guys you sent over are asking some weird questions, we'd like to talk with you about this. What's the deal?'' Maskela was on the scene within the hour.

"And who are these men?''

"We were told that you were sending them to us.''

"Who did you speak to about this?''

They exchanged dum-dum looks, suddenly realizing that they were mere amateurs in the game. Mr. Amos Maskela of the Central Committee, was firm and clear. "You must be careful, my friends, the Boers are ingenious, they have enlisted many different kinds of people to help them maintain Apartheid. They will do anything to maintain their slave system.''

He left them with several pieces of advice, the primary one being, 'don't trust anyone until they have been validated.'

The invitation from Marcus Tambolu to come to 'a small gathering of friends' was irresistible.

"What do you think it means, Kuumba?''

"I think it means we're being invited to a 'small gathering of friends,' that's what the brother said.''

'A small gathering of friends' featured Zena as the

151

centerpiece. Tony wasn't surprised by her appearance at first, not 'til the impact hit. This was Marcus Tambolu's wife, the mother of his son.

"Hello Tony, Kuumba. I'm glad you could come." She spoke in a firm, resigned voice, pretending to be indifferent to Tony's attitude towards her.

"Yes, politics do make strange *bedfellows,* don't they?" She ignored his remark, made an oblique move and was off to talk with a distinguished looking Indian couple in the far corner.

"Tony, Tony," Kuumba whispered, "I understand how you feel, man, but you can't come up in here, insultin' peoples' wives 'n shit."

"Yeah, I know. I'm cool. I just couldn't resist that one."

The so-called party was a gathering of ANC people and sympathizers. It was an agony for Tony because of Zena. She seemed to be everywhere he turned and she was more beautiful than she'd ever been. He stood off to the side, one pint, staring at her. As usual she was wearing one of her dramatic, but simple outfits, a wide white skirt and a mint green blouse. Whenever she caught his eye, she stared back, returned the challenging look. Marcus Tambolu arrived suddenly at the peak of the social chit chat.

"My friends, I thank you for being here this evening." He spoke in a conversational tone that was heard in every corner of the large room, he was the center of attention. "I will make my remarks brief and to the point. All of us here are deeply involved in the struggle to free South Africa from the vicious Apartheid system. We have much work to do.

"Some of us may not live to see the objective accomplished, but that should not affect our desires to do what has to be done." He bowed slightly after his five minute impromptu speech, cast his sad little smile at them and strolled out with Zena on his arm, flanked by two

152

bodyguards.

Activities at the Jazz Zimbabwe picked up immediately after the party. The club became an Underground Railroad for guerrillas, refugees, businessmen/women, hitmen/women, people trying to destroy Apartheid.

"Kuumba, you now something, man, our country is full of shit." Kuumba looked up from the keyboard and smiled at his friend.

"So what else have you discovered today?"

"I'm serious man. Check it out. We have people coming through here who've been trained in damned near every right thinking country in the world, except ours."

"That's racism at work, pal."

"But the Soviet Union is racist. China is racist, the Bulgarians..."

"Yeah, I know," Kuumba spun around on the piano bench, "They also have some sense of what the deal is. They know they're going to have to deal with the African people as soon as the Afrikaners are booted out of the box, so they're making some kind of contribution now, to be able to say, 'hey, remember us, we helped you when you were down.'"

"Why doesn't the U.S. government do that?"

"'Cause they keep bringing one racist government in after another, usually with a racist at the head. Reaganism, on the racist level, will be with us for a helluva long time. To make a long story short, the government of our country, over the years has always been blinded by racist attitudes.

"If they haven't revised all the history books in the school systems to say that America was *not* 'discovered' by the Europeans, then I know that racism is the heart of this belief that white people are entitled to lie about everybody's history.

"That's why our government has always been caught on the wrong side; Marcos, the Thuis, Trujillo, Pappy Doc and the Baby. They don't have to necessarily be white, but they

153

should have the European's self interest at heart, even if they ain't realized it.''

Kuumba turned back, to the piano.

"It's a fucked up situation. We could wind up with a worldwide overthrow of all white powers, even in white countries, by so called minorities. They have to protect each other.

"I tried to cool a lot of it out with my music, but we have some people in this world who believe sheer noise is music. What do you do with them?''

Tony and Kuumba became involved with other lives. Matthew Motlana came into their lives, he was one of the people who had escaped from the South African secret police and was returning to kill Apartheid. they shard a fifth of rum with him after the Jazz Zimbabwe shut down for the night.

"You can't dismantle slavery, you have to kill it.'' Motlana was making his fifth sabotage trip into South Africa. "I have blown up radio stations in Pretoria, bombed police stations in Joh'berg, assassinated high officials, terrorized white conclaves in Joh'berg, with guerrilla attacks and never felt guilty. You can't dismantle a machine put together with that much precision. You must blow it up so that the pieces cannot be put back together, ever.''

They absorbed the sense of what he as saying and tried to fit it within the context of their own African-American experience.

"No, Kuumba, Tony, you cannot really compare the two experiences. The Boer and your white man are quite different. Your white man surrendered to the inevitable before you reached the point of an all out race war because he knows he would have lost. They knew, if you weren't destroyed by raw slavery, it would be impossible to do you in now.''

Tony eased in, "You're not quite right, Matthew. "Our

white man didn't surrender, he went underground and took all of this apparatus with him. It may seem that our "Boer" is different from your Boer, but he's not. He's just a little more subtle.

Kuumba popped in, as though on cue, "Matthew, what you have to remember is that oppression can be even more profound when it doesn't seem to exist on the raw blatant funky level. Can you dig where I'm coming from? In the States, no matter how poor we are, they will always allot us a certain number of television sets per ghetto, to maintain our ignorance at a certain level, and make certain that we are always divided. That's an example of a certain kind of oppression."

"But they're not real Boers," Matthew Motlana protested, "People with a mentality that is so dense that they cannot see the inevitable. He is a savage beast who wants to grind our bones to dust."

"Matthew," Tony shot back, "you're right, up to a certain point. Our 'Boers,' our white men, have a different mentality because of the peculiarities of his history. I guarantee you that they have much more in common than they seem to have."

"Matthew, check it out," Kuumba played follow up, "our Boers started off with the native girls, same as yours did. They raped, lied and bullshitted. They were both neurotic and they haven't changed a helluva lot. I suspect the only difference between your Boer and our Boer is that yours wants to openly carry slavery into the 21st century, ours wants to sneak it in."

"Yes, my friends, you are right. They have much in common. Can I tell you what a Boer, one of our so called enlightened Boers, once told me? I will never forget it.

"'Listen, Motlana,' he said, 'Apartheid might appear to be bad, but in reality, it may have been one of the best things to ever happen to your people. It taught you to be on time.'"

"'Whose time?' I asked him. He had me framed and I did two years in jail for speaking to him in that manner. That definitely radicalized me. Imagine a man having another man jailed for speaking? I hate them and wish they were all dead, that we could eliminate their ugly memories from our minds.

"Can you imagine the psychologists and psychiatrists who are needed now? That we don't have. You can begin to understand the need for such people after we've come to power. Many millions have been wounded by a psychological atom bomb that exploded on our minds for hundreds of years.

"Yes, brothers, we must be some strong souls."

"Matthew, what would happen to you if they caught you?"

"They would probably torture me. They love to torture Black people. I think we are a sexual turn on for them in some way. They are trapped, with no place to go and like a paranoid partner, he wants to keep beating me up.

"I don't know where they got the notion we would accept that, we never have, none of us."

The Jazz Zimbabwe Club became the spot to meet for your intrigue. ANC meetings in the basement 'til dawn, secret messages transmitted in musical codes, fiery articles from Tony.

"I can't believe any magazine would pay me to explain why Apartheid isn't acceptable. Do you?"

"If you were listening to me closely the other night, you would remember what I told you about the American government being in love with racism. And that magazine is an extension of the government."

Zena made infrequent appearances, accompanying Marcus Tambolu. Tony felt drained from the effort of controlling his feelings.

"Kuumba, what am I going to do about this situation, man? Just when I thing I've put a cap on my emotions, this woman

156

shows up and I feel like I'm about to melt."

"Hey, brother man, I've given you all the advice I can give you. It's on you now."

Bulawayo was filled with excitement from many different sources. The anticipated war with South Africa, the ebb and flow of international events that seemed to center on what was taking place in Bulawayo, the racial madness of the 21st century was happening in Bulawayo.

Tony sat back at his desk, a ballpoint behind is ear, two on the desk. How in the hell can I put this together? My stupid love for this woman, her marriage to one of the biggies in the ANC, being in Africa, in a war, wanting her so much that I feel empty whenever I think of her and realize that we're in the same part of the world. At least we have that much. But why me?

He strolled from his office-writing room to get a bottle of cognac from behind the long bar of the club. He surprised Kuumba and one of the beautiful sisters of Bulawayo, a city well known for the special beauty of their women, having a midnight chat in the a distant corner. Tony felt a sudden spark of jealously. Why are things so easy for him and so hard for me?

"Tony, come over here, brother. I want to introduce you to a friend." Tony moved through the forest of tables, doing a close up study of the woman as he got closer. Thirty-ish, fashionably dressed in an eclectic African-European blend, black as a panther, sleek, hip. They had to be hip to deal with Kuumba. He had said many times, 'I cannot cope with an unhip woman, I simply cannot do it. She must not only be hip, but she must be authentically hip. It's nothing you can put your finger on, it just simply must be there.'

"Tony Nia Jones, my partner, meet Letta Mugabe." Tony suddenly felt self-conscious holding a fifth of cognac by the neck. Kuumba, always ready for a little teasing, flicked his eyes from Tony's eyes to the bottle of cognac.

"Looks like you're getting ready to go off 'n do a lil' solitary boozin', brother."

Tony felt insulted, defensive. "Hey, I'm a grown man. I can get drunk if I want to."

The woman watched the exchange with sly eyes, a subtle smile curling the corners of her mouth.

"I didn't say you couldn't get drunk, partner. I just made an observation. No need to get pissed." The woman's sly eyes fixed him with a bold stare. Kuumba took note and approved of the flirtation. Tony looks like a haunted man, I guess he was right, she does haunt him. He needs to let up on himself.

"No problem. Guess I'm just feeling a little out of it. You know how it is."

"Sure you don't want to sit down and have a little taste with me and Miss Mugabe?"

"Yes, please join us," she insisted and reached her hand out to him. He was surprised by her firm grip on his hand. It felt odd. African women, like most women everywhere he'd been, seemed to treat the handshake as a male thing.

He eased in beside her, making her the centerpiece. "Well, I'm here and I brought my own bottle."

She was gorgeous to look at and smelled like some rare flower up close. Kuumba moved his glass over for a shot of cognac. Miss Mugabe refused a drink.

"I only drink water, only water."

Kuumba took it up. It was one of their favorite things, or had been until Zena came along, to meet and have fun with beautiful women. It was subtle, witty fun and the result and often resulted in a menage a trois. "Now just a minute Miss Mugabe, are you going to tell me that you've denied yourself the pleasure of Coca Cola, Orange Crush, root beer, not to mention a good St. Julien '68?" Kuumba settled back, feeling mellow, enjoying the company of good people.

"Well, Mr. Jones, it might seem that I've been denied these pleasures, but it certainly hasn't hurt my body or my disposition."

"Oweeee! That was mean, Letta, I mean *mean*."

The woman looked puzzled. Black Americans had such a strange sense of humor. Tony felt himself sinking into a game he really didn't feel like playing. "Miss Mugave, it's been a pleasure to meet you. I look forward to seeing you again and talking with you."

Kuumba felt cheated. He had looked forward to the tripling up. Oh well.

"Talk to you later, buddy."

"Yeah, we'll rap later on."

He left them to return to his own turf. There was not further need to try to be warm and witty. He knew Kuumba would understand.

"Your friend seems to be very troubled."

"You got that right. Can I get you another Perrier?"

Tony propped himself behind his desk and poured himself a large cognac, downed it, poured another one and sipped it. He took the ballpoint from behind his ear and scribbled on the pad, 'I love Zena.' And felt like screaming and crying at the same time. The conflicting emotions seemed to cancel each other out, leaving him feeling numb. He sprawled in his seat, mentally reviewing his relationship to this exotic woman who had come into his life and changed it forever.

Zena, Zena, Zena, the name alone forced hundreds of delicious thoughts through his head. God, it was so beautiful, so sweet. The nights in Rio when we made love for hours, almost torturing each other with pleasure. He poured another dollop of cognac into his glass. What a cruel place this world can be. Scenes of Rio flashed through his consciousness as his pen stirred around in the air, searching for a beginning.

159

Maybe it was the night we did the samba at the neighborhood block party all night. Or was it the afternoon we simply surrendered our emotional basements to each other? Or at least one of us did.

The slow, sour taste of her betrayal, of the note at the airport saying, 'I won't be with you,' made him scowl. The sound of his private phone ringing, refused to register in his consciousness for a couple beats. Who would be calling me this late?

"Hello?"

"Hello, Tony, this is Zena."

What the hell is this? Kuumba must be playing some kind of joke. "Zena, is it really you?" he couldn't control the waver in his voice.

Her voice sounded cold, distant. "Yes, it is. One moment please, Marcus wants to speak with you." He ground his teeth together. She goes from being the mirage in a fantasy to bitter reality. He felt tempted to slam the phone back into its cradle.

"Tony Jones, Marcus Tambolu here." What should I say, 'yessuh boss?'

"Yes Marcus, what can I do for you?" He could hear an undercurrent of conversation in the background. Must be having another one of those around-the-clock-sessions.

"We have an assignment for you and Kuumba." How ironic, the man who's married to the woman I love gives me orders.

"What is it?"

"I can't tell you over the phone. A messenger is on his way to you."

"We'll be on the lookout."

They hung up simultaneously, no good-byes, attempts to be jolly. Tony felt frustrated angry, rotten. She calls me to have me speak with her man. He poured another slug of

160

cognac into his glass. Wonder what he wants us to do? Anything would be better than sitting around here waiting . . .

He shuffled to the door, slightly buzzed. Kuumba and Miss Mugabe were practically talking into each other's faces across the table.

"Kuumba, give me a minute, will you?"

The couple looked at him, annoyed. "It won't take but a minute."

"Be right back, Letta, hold your point."

Tony led him to a far corner of the club. "I just talked to Marcus Tambolu. they're sending a messenger over with some stuff for us to do."

Kuumba's eyes lit up. "Any idea what it is?"

"Not the slightest. I just thought I'd alert you just in case you planned to slip out for a bit."

"Well, I certainly was planning to, I'm not going to deny that."

"She sho' is fine, bro' . . ."

"Yeah, she is, ain't she." They exchanged coded, chauvinistic smiles.

"In any case, a messenger from Tambolu is on the way. Stick around."

"No problem, not at all. I'll let him in when he comes." They returned to their respective areas; Kuumba to say a few more words to his lady; Tony to drink, brood and write. Here I am, a free, independent African-American man, being led around by the nose by my woman's husband. The cognac welled up in his throat, tasting sour. He heard the knocking at the door and stared out of the office. Kuumba cut him off.

"I'll get it."

Tony stood in the door of his office, his eyes on Kuumba's back, idly wondering what they were going to be asked to do. The crack of the pistols didn't register for a split second, only the image of Kuumba crumpling in the door like a wet rag.

Two gunman squatted in the doorway of the club and sprayed the interior with automatic weapon fire. Tony scrambled back to his office, crawling across the floor to reach the Uzi in the bottom drawer of his desk. By the time he reached his piece the assassins had jumped into a waiting car and sped away.

He raced to the door to spray a few rounds at the car. Letta Mugabe was bending over Kuumba, crying silently.

"I think he's dead."

Tony couldn't stop himself from laughing. Somehow, he felt, Kuumba was saying something sarcastic like, 'You're damned right I'm dead, how would you feel if you'd been shot twelve times?' Tony felt the blood drain from his head. Kuumba isn't dead. He couldn't be dead. Kuumba is my best friend, the baddest piano player on the planet. The sirens screeching suddenly, the police cars careening to a stop, the hard questions. "Are you related to the deceased, suh?" forced him to accept the fact of his friend's death.

Bulawayo buzzed the next day. An Afrikaner murder squad had hit the city. Tony left the police station, after a night and half a day of answering questions, speeding to ANC headquarters.

Twenty minutes later, he stood in front of bombed out two story building, pock marked with heavy caliber gunfire. Amos Masekela turned a corner, pursued by a forest of video cameras. He paused in front of the ruined building, impatiently answered questions for ten minutes.

Tony caught his eye and signalled to him that he wanted to speak with him. Masekela, shook himself free of the reporters and strode to a waiting car, signalling for Tony to come with him.

"I'm driving, why don't I follow you?" He followed Masekela's car through the outraged streets of Bulawayo.

Tony felt nauseated. Bulawayo, with its neatly laid out avenues, manicured lawns and attractive shops suddenly seemed ominous, oppressive. The block that Marcus Tambolu lived on when he was in town was sealed off. They were forced to park two blocks away.

The neat two story English Tudor home, surrounded by neatly trimmed hedges, was gutted. Tony stared at the smoking rubble, the devastation. Masekela seemed to be looking for someone as he spoke.

"Those bloody bastards!"

"What happened?"

"As clearly as we've been able to put it together, a South African kamikaze squad..."

"Kamikaze?"

"Yes, kamikaze, because they knew they wouldn't be able to do this and escape. And fortunately, none of them did. They started their raids about 2:00 am last night, striking five locations simultaneously. Your place was one of the designated targets. I am very sorry about Kuumba."

A man in a tattered shirt and threadbare trousers walked over to Tony and Masekela, tears glistening on his dark cheeks. "They got him," she said, without a change of expression. Tony grabbed his arm.

"They got who?"

"They got our leader, Marcus Tambolu."

Tony and Masekela stared at the man. "Are you sure?" Tony probed.

"I helped bring the bodies out this morning."

Masekela seemed to be making calculations, his jaw muscles twitching. "Are you positive?" he snapped suddenly.

"Yes, I am positive," the man answered.

"Bodies? How many? Whose bodies?" Tony asked. The man backed away from them a few steps as though the

163

information he had was too harsh to give them close up.

"Only the child is alive, and he is badly injured."

"Who are you talking about, man?!" Tony heard himself yell at the man. The man calmly stared into his eyes and began to count off the number that they had pulled from the rubble.

"We pulled five from the first floor, all men; Marcus Tambolu, a woman and the little boy from the second floor."

"Where is the boy?! Where did they take him?!"

"To Bulawayo General Hospital."

Tony started running to his car. My son is alive! My son is alive! My son...

He sat at his son's bedside for long, tortured hours, listening to a stream of sophisticated medical jargon concerning his condition, until he finally decided to punch through to his version of reality.

"Look Doc, let's cut the medical bullshit. What's happening with my son?"

"Your son, sir?"

"Yes, my son..."

"But, his name is Tambolu?"

"It's a long story. What's the real deal?"

"Well, we've done all we can. We think he'll live but he's in for a long convalescence. He has two badly fractured legs, a severe concussion..."

"But he'll live?"

"Yes, and with God's help, he'll be a healthy young man, but it's going to take a great deal of care."

Tony petitioned the ANC Welfare Committee for guardianship of Marcus Tambolu's son. Brother Amos Maskela and Matthew Motlana, aware of the true story Tambolu's 'son,' became valuable allies.

"We believe in the extended family, an we know that you have the boy's best interests at heart and that he will be well

164

cared for.''

The club was closed temporarily to give Tony more time to make arrangements for his son's care and for him to regroup. Letta Mugabe became his friend.

"Tony, if I can help you in any way, please call.''

The suicide squad, all killed and accounted for, was traced to a minor league South African agency, euphemistically named 'Bureau of Claims.'

Tony, sitting at the end of the long table fixed his stare on the flushed pink faces of the Afrikaner negotiators. They gave him the impression of being creatures from another world, literally. The Afrikaners were attempting to pressure the ANC and all of the groups participating in the negotiation process to grant them as many of the privileges as they had been forced to relinquish after the Apartheid regime had been beaten. It was unreal. The Boers had been defeated by the people they had oppressed, they had been overthrown and yet they hoped to maintain their position by appealing to the African sense of decency.

"Can't you people understand? If we are asked to become mere symbols of what we used to be, we could wind up being the Palestinians of Africa.''

Tony eased away from the long table, indicating to Amos Masekela and Matthew Motlana that he was taking a much needed break from the Afrikaner rhetoric. The Literary Committee of the ANC had commissioned him to do a version of the proceedings, their version. The responsibility weighed him down. And, from time to time, he had to take breaks. He strolled out of the conference room, packed with television cameras, newspaper reporters and other people who were seriously interested in the future of southern Africa. He wandered through the corridor onto the tenth story glass enclosed terrace of the Cafe Johannesburg, formerly

165

reserved for whites only.

"Your order, please, suh?"

He stared at the smooth, dark mooned face, smiling down at him. "Make it a double cognac." He redirected his stare onto the buildings of downtown Johannesburg. It was the tenth anniversary of Marcus Tambolu's murder and African Azania was preparing a smorgasbord of memorial services. It was not universally celebrated by the Europeans, nor appreciated, but they had no choice but to accept the anniversary as a fact of life.

He sipped his cognac, thoughtfully playing one of his mental tapes, backwards. Ten years ago. Ten short years ago. Ten years ago I lost my best friend, the only woman I've ever loved was murdered, the man who persuaded me to join the struggle was murdered, my son was wounded. Many thousands have spent years of their lives in jails, thousands were murdered. And now we sit at a conference table with the murderers, trying to work out some kind of agreement that will allow peaceful coexistence to develop and equal treatment under the law.

He sipped his cognac, trying to block the flow of memories, some beautiful, Zena in Rio; some ugly, Kuumba crumpling in the doorway of the club.

Zena. No matter how subliminal the memories were, whenever her presence flowed back into his consciousness he was forced to linger there, an emotional miser counting his gold ducats in the darkness.

Zena. I think we would have had a beautiful life together, if circumstances had allowed it to happen.

Letta Mugabe had made a valiant effort to fill an emotional void. "You've lost the woman you love and I have lost the man I was beginning to love." They fell into each other's arms by default and remained locked in place for a year, sharing a love-grief. And when it was over they became

166

friends for life.

In addition, Letta Mugabe's family became Marcus Tambolu II's extended family, in between the twelve operations he suffered through, a harbor for him.

Tony felt old at thirty-six, tired, wounded. The armed struggle was over, the negotiations lingered. After Mandela's release, the Apartheid regime was beaten by a combination of nation crippling strikes, armed struggle, international pressures and African persistence.

The die hard Boers still called Azania, South Africa, as though nothing had happened, as though the society they lived in (those who hadn't fled to the United States, Israel, Portugal, England, Argentina and Australia) had been turned upside down.

He felt anger, too, aside from everything else, toward the generosity the Africans were extending to the Afrikaners.

"Man, I really don't understand it, I have to admit."

"Tony, please understand that we hate the Boers as much as any living creature on Earth. Look what he did to us, made us the last slaves in the world. But we promised to be fair and if we're not, if we discredited ourselves and lined them up against the wall, we would be lower than they were. We don't want revenge, what kind of revenge would be suitable for what they did to us?"

He smiled in confusion, overwhelmed by the idea that he was present at the dawn of a new history. Some intelligent, humane people were going to be given the opportunity that they had fought for. Why me? He asked himself at least once a day. He had planned to duff out, market what he had learned over a ten year period, fighting Apartheid.

Mathabane and the other respected Azanian writers had nothing new to tell him, he had already experienced it ahead of time. They called it segregation then, his grandmother told him all about it.

"They treated us worse than dogs, Tony, worse than dogs."

The Afrikaners argued that they were going to become, 'Palestinians,' people with a name but no homeland. They were offered the homelands, the Bantustans or a place in Azanian society, if they met the proper criteria. A few of the realists jumped on the wagon right away.

Mandela's successor explained, "The Boers will always have a place in Azania but not as rulers. They are simply one of the minor tribes of the nation."

They were forced to understand, but still resisted. There were even Afrikaner guerrilla bands on the outskirts of Pretoria. The United States and Israel, two of the last bastions of subtle racism in the world, had finally convinced the Boers of South Africa that they should join the ranks of the has beens. Line up behind England, maybe. President Westing, a reincarnation of Eisenhower, from years ago, was appointed spokesman for the official de-gradation of the Boers of South Africa. They offered their total acceptance of conditions but declined to believe the unbelievable, South Africa had become Azania. Thousands of Afrikaners committed suicide after the results of the first national election were counted.

Matthew Motlana, slumped into the seat beside Tony, signalling the waitress for a drink at the same time. "They are an unbelievable bunch, these fucking Boers." He mimicked a man spitting out at a distant spittoon. "They are still arguing for a separate state in Azania. We've offered them any of the Bantustans they'd like to go to, if they were good enough for us, then they ought to be good enough for them."

Tony sipped and looked thoughtfully into his friends face.

"Matthew, my brother, that's what made them Boers. They never thought about how you felt. We had crackers in the South and the North who felt exactly the same way. Your Boers lynched you all legally, constitutionally, ours actually did it physically, whenever they got the chance. Let's get on back in there and see how this thing is working out.''

Motlana canceled his drink and followed Tony back to the conference room. Security was tight. They were re-validated three times before they got to the conference room. Tony gritted his teeth as he re-entered the room and stared at the moist pink faces sitting on the far side of the conference table. These dirty, rotten motherfuckers. If I had my way, I'd line 'em up against the walls in Soweto and shoot them down like dogs. He felt deep admiration for the Azanians. They had developed into a super people. The oppression had fashioned/ironed out an African that was almost superhuman. They had endured and overcome so much on the basis of having sheer willpower and direct access to their melanin sources.

The Boers had never been able to get into what made the Africans tick. There were even reports that the government laboratories had dissected living Africans to look for the mysterious element that enabled them to overcome so much oppression.

Tony rested his arms on the polished table face and stared at the Boers representatives. They reminded him of a statement he had once read about Hitler's henchmen. ''The thing that is frightening about them is their ordinariness. It is difficult to imagine how such ordinary men could be guilty of such extraordinary crimes.'' He scribbled notes in his notebook. They are fiends of the most perverse kind. They don't deserve to be offered options, given humane considerations. There were Azanians who did want revenge for what they had suffered under the Apartheid regime and from time to time, they surfaced fully blown.

There were several bizarre cases of Azanians forcing

Afrikaner families into slavery, others were simply shot to death by revenge seekers. They were promptly punished by the new government, honoring their promise to world peace groups that there would be no racial blood baths. Contrary to the propaganda that the Afrikaners had saturated the media with, saying that tribal warfare was completely predictable, there was not widespread violence between the tribes when emancipation was achieved.

All the people of color became Azanians, including those Afrikaners who qualified for citizenship. The Azanians were trying to do the right thing. They were determined to follow the precepts of their national character. The people shall govern. All national groups shall have equal rights under the law. The people shall share in the country's wealth. The people are entitled to and shall enjoy equal human rights. All people shall be allowed to do rewarding work and granted security from police harassment. Schools shall be free and open to all applicants. The people shall be entitled to houses and all of the creature comforts that the nation can help provide. There shall be peace and friendship internally. And finally, the African people of Azania shall have control of the country called Azania forever. The last chapter, subtitled "the African people of Azania" was the bone that the Boers couldn't get out of their throats.

Tony forced himself to record the early work of the reconstruction as objectively as possible. The days stretched into weeks, months and finally, after a year, he was able to give the ANC negotiating committee the first draft of 'Anzania Now.'

Tony smiled at his son's sleeping profile. He looks so much like his mother. They were on their way home, to America. Tony went back to the lounge for a drink, to re-fuel himself for the next barrage of questions from Marcus Tambolu II.

"What is America like, Uncle Tony?"

"Uncle Tony." He had asked Amos Masekela for advice about the problem of pretending to be his son's uncle. "Tony, there is a time for him to learn the truth, when he gets older, better able to deal with the hard facts of the world."

"Uncle Tony."

He returned to his seat feeling that urge to have his feet on solid land after so many hours in the air.

"Uncle Tony, what were you starting to tell me about America, before I went to sleep?"

"Awake again, huh?"

"Yes, I'm awake again."

Tony liked his son's direct approach to things, but he seemed to lack a sense of humor. Everything was taken seriously. He attributed the trait to all of the years the young man was operated on, forced to remain immobile while the surgery to correct his fractured legs healed.

"Well, as I recall, I was telling you why the Europeans were so anxious to convert all of the Native Americans and the enslaved Africans to Christianity. Christianity, you see, as promoted by the Europeans was a clever way of making the oppressed and enslaved feel as though they had a chance for a better life in the next world, or the next life. They designed a master role for themselves to play and gave everybody else supporting roles to play and justified it with the Bible."

"Are they still trying to do that?"

Tony hesitated, measuring the depths he could get into with a precocious fourteen year old. "I hate to say it, Marcus, but its still true. The only difference is that the Bible has been exchanged for gold plated charge cards, diamonds and expensive cars. It's been years since I've been back home, but I've kept up to date."

"Uncle Tony, does the segregation that you told me about

171

still exist?''

Was segregation still alive and thriving in the U.S.?

"Yes, Marcus, segregation is still in existence. It's disguised better than ever but its still there. The racism that gave the first European invaders the nerve to plant their flags all over the place and claim that they had ''discovered'' a new land is still there. Marcus, what you have to understand about the racist mentality is that it never dies. Sometimes, its forced underground, but its always there. If it existed in the beginning you can damn sure bet it's going to exist in the end.''

"But why, Uncle Tony, why?''

He felt in tune with the despair, the anguish in the boy's question. "It would take years to fully explain why some people have to justify rippin' other people off because they happen to be another color. Racism is a European invention, in the same way that Apartheid was an Afrikaner invention.''
He looked out at the cloud banks. He had used Marcus as the motivation for coming back to take a long, hard look at his country. He wanted his son to experience what was happening and to understand what was happening in the belly of the beast.

The outline of New York's skyline sent sudden chills up and down his back. He was back home.

The plane circled to land, making him feel weak knowing what he'd have to face and/or deal with the minute the plane landed. The clever lies, the racist bullshit that was disguised by having everything wrapped in the flag and calling it democracy. Or patriotism.

"Marcus, let me drop down to the bottom line on you and say this. The people of color in this world have had to constantly fight off the European obsession to dominate us and it doesn't seem that things are ever going to change.''

"Not ever, Uncle Tony.''

172

Sweat trickled freely under Tony's armpits and the urge to lie swelled up in him.

"No, Marcus, they are not ever going to change, which means that we must never let our guard down."

"Not ever?"

"No, Marcus, not ever."

Dear Zena, I love you always, Tony.

It took me a long, long time to discover that Tony Nia Jones was my real father. It didn't take me quite so long to discover his real feelings about America.

He was typical, I think in some ways, of a lot of the men and women of his generation. He wasn't exactly bitter about his experience as an African-American writer, but there was an edge to the way he talked about it.

"This place ain't never gave me shit, I've always had to take it!"

We didn't see the same Americans. He looked at it from the vantage point of an expatriate reluctantly returning. I saw it as an exciting new place, filled with all kinds of wild stuff to do.

We returned to Tony's home, Chicago. He couldn't remain "Uncle" Tony and after I found out he was my real father at sixteen or so, it was too late to attach "Dad" to him.

Tony's family couldn't really figure the situation out, they were straight forward, down home folks.

"Tony, whose child is this? He's the spittin' image of you. And what's this stuff about "Uncle" Tony?"

It was revealed to me like that, in bits 'n pieces 'n slices.

I did look like "Uncle" Tony, and not at all like Marcus Tambolu, my "father."

"Now, Tony, you say this is the son of that man Tambolu?"

"Uncle" Tony finally had to give it up. His Aunt Esther

and her husband were the catalysts. "That boy oughta know the truth about himself."

And the visits from home forced it into play; Ms. Letta Mugabe, the Director of the Zimbabwe Textile Industry, came to visit. It was obvious that the two of them shared something very deep.

She spent a week in Chicago, doing business for her country, and looking strangely at me.

Matthew Motlana, Amos Masekela and a number of other people who had been politically active, came to our house.

And I always thought they smiled oddly at me when I was introduced as Marcus Tambolu II.

I give Tony credit, he held on for as long as he could. And then one night, while we were at a Phavia Kujichagulia performance, he broke down and started crying, talking about his partner, Theolonius Kuumba Brown.

We went backstage to see sister Kujichagulia and it happened there. They talked about the piano player as though he were still alive.

"Tony, you know how he makes these runs, trippin' up 'n down the keys? Rippling thru everything from 'Mary had a Little Lamb' to Miles Davis' 'Kind of Blue.'"

"Yeah, that's one of his trademarks."

Sister Kujichagulia could do that with Tony, talk in the present tense about someone who was past. They only did that when they talked about Master Brown.

She was on her way to a gig in Mandela City, South Africa, and from there to Switzerland and from there to God only knows. The woman was serious about taking her message to the world.

"Tony, how does it feel to be the father of a boy named Marcus Tambolu?"

She didn't jive around, and you could tell from the curl of her lip that she meant for him to be straight with me.

174

That's when he broke down and started talking to me about it, she went on for her last show of the evening. We remained backstage.

"I loved Zena, your mother, in a way that not many men know how to love anymore. Its all instant now, here today, exit tomorrow.

And she loved me too, even though she was married to Tambolu. I aided and abetted the marriage because Tambolu was a very, very important man for Africa, and maybe for the world, at that point in time.

I loved her enough to want to see her make another man's life complete. I felt the sacrifice was worth it. But obviously I didn't commit my total energies to the project.

He hugged me, something he did frequently, like a body handshake.

"I'm glad we had you, you're like a link to her."

Something happened between us that night. I felt closer in spirit. Tony Nia Jones, with his partner, Theolonius Seminole Kuumba Brown, had tripped out into the world when they were young men, had wandered around the world, done things, helped revolutions happen, were influential.

I felt proud to be his son, and to be Marcus Tambolu's son, and Zena's son. Marcus Tambolu began to mean more to me in some way, after I discovered who I was.

Genetically, I was in the best of all possible worlds. I had the spiritual shadow of Marcus Tambolu covering my back, beautiful, brainy, ethereal Zena was my mother, married to and buried with Marcus, and Tony was my father.

After the opening revelation, he took me through the whole emotional flavor of the times. With each day, after every session, I understood a little better why he felt about America the way he did.

I didn't share his opinions totally. But I understood a little better.

175

I wasn't prepared to see him die, I think I was more surprised than grieved.

He got sick suddenly, went thru an intense period of being well and got sick again. They diagnosed cancer of this and that. I think it was something else.

He was sixty and I don't think he could take the changes the world was going through.

"Dammit! I told those fools in "Scars and Memories" what the deal had always been, but they saw it as the story of somebody's life. Maybe the picture on the cover was misleading.

"O well, fuck it, its too late to worry about shit like that now."

He was struck down in his prime. Aside from the cancer, his ears had given out almost but otherwise he was whole.

He liked wine, women and song. And when we had his funeral, all were in evidence.

I've been thinking about writing his story, I think I'd call it "One Love," to celebrate what he and mom shared.

Yeahh, I think I might do that as soon as I finish this play.

I should call Simone . . .